Frozen In Time

Frozen In Time © Copyright 2004 by Ron Hutson

Cover design by Katgraphics@ntlworld.com

Cover picture by permission of Norfolk County Council Library and Information Service

All rights reserved. No part of this work may be reproduced or stored in an information retrieval system (other than for purposes of review) without prior written permission by the copyright holder.

A catalogue record of this book is available from the British Library

First Edition: November 2004

ISBN: 1-84375-122-4

This is a work of fiction. Names, characters, places and incidents are the product of the author's imagination or are used fictitiously, and any resemblance to any actual persons, living or dead, events, or locales is entirely coincidental.

To order additional copies of this book please visit:
http://www.upso.co.uk/ronhutson

Published by: UPSO Ltd
5 Stirling Road, Castleham Business Park,
St Leonards-on-Sea, East Sussex TN38 9NW United Kingdom
Tel: 01424 853349 Fax: 0870 191 3991
Email: info@upso.co.uk Web: http://www.upso.co.uk

Frozen In Time

by

Ron Hutson

UPSO

To my wife, partner and friend for over forty years

Acknowledgements

To my grandchildren, Maria and Georgina for
searching the Internet

Part 1

Early March 1961

Chapter 1

The train from Norwich to Cromer and Sheringham pulled in at the station of Worstead, the stop before the market town of North Walsham. Three people alighted, a man and a woman together, familiar with the place, headed straight off the platform, across the level crossing which opened over the tracks as soon as the train left, and along the country road, presumably to home, though no houses were in sight. The third person, a young man of 21, neatly dressed in suit and tie, was not so sure of his surroundings. I had not been here before but must have passed through on day trips to the coast as a child. I looked around before heading to the exit to show my ticket to the porter. As I passed the waiting room window I saw my reflection, quickly took out my comb to make sure no hair was out of place, straightened my tie and left the station. Across the road was the factory with it's name 'Westwick Frozen Foods' across the entrance. I took a letter from my inside pocket, gave it a reassuring glance, put it back, crossed the road and began to walk down the drive to the factory buildings.

The boundary between Westwick and Worstead isn't clear. Worstead is about a mile to the east of the station that bears it's name. It's just a small hamlet with shop, post office, butchers and pub around the village square, but it boasts a truly magnificent 13th century church of St. Mary, huge and out of proportion to the size of the village, yet a sign of a once very prosperous community, for Worstead gave it's name to the cloth 'Worsted' woven many years ago by Flemish weavers when this area profited from the wool trade. The yarn was spun from long-fibred wool which was combed, not carded and was popular for warm men's suits. The huge church benefited from the gratitude and generosity of the then wealthy, church-going community.

Westwick, on the other hand, seems to have no obvious centre. It meanders across country to the west of Worstead and is famous for it's cherry orchards that belong to Westwick Hall and sell their fruit by the roadside in season, and for the famous Westwick Arch which straddles the Norwich to North Walsham road. With it's three, pointed, Gothic style windows on each side and it's Classical triangular pediment, this magnificent arch marks the entrance to the Westwick Estate.

Between the two, sits Westwick Frozen Food Factory, and a vacancy had arisen for a food technician in the factory's laboratory. That was the reason for myself, John Clark being here. My appointment was for 11am and I was in good time but I was both hopeful and apprehensive: apprehensive because I had no experience of what the job entailed and hopeful that they wouldn't notice. The advert hadn't specified other than 3 'O'levels and a willingness to learn. I had 6 'O' levels which must count for something, though I had failed at art, but I hoped that wouldn't count. I was also hopeful that this might be the chance to get out of the tedium of working for the Inland Revenue, Norwich 'B' Collection. I wasn't cut out to spend my day cajoling and threatening people into paying their overdue taxes. Of course somebody had to do it but I didn't want it to be me. I'd already had a warning from my senior officer a Miss Belsham that I must be firmer when on the phone to dilatory payers but I was too soft, that was my problem, believing every sob story I heard. It's a wonder I didn't offer to pay their taxes for them sometimes. Miss Belsham on the other hand could get manure out of a rocking horse, and never seemed to miss seeing anything from her office overlooking the main office. Her initials were B.D. and someone had said they should be B.D.I.-Beady -eye-Belsham.

The factory office was at the end of a curving drive, away from the railway, on the right. The factory buildings were to the left. Sliding doors were open to let forklift trucks enter and leave and there was a hive of activity about the place as people went about their business, most wearing long white coats and white hats. There was a pervading smell of vegetation but it wasn't possible to identify the actual food source. The reception desk was manned by a young woman seated behind a typewriter and when I announced my name and the purpose of my visit, showing her my interview appointment, she asked me to wait whilst she informed the factory manager. Two minutes later he arrived, a stocky man in a white coat wearing a trilby type, white hat which I was later to discover was the prerogative of senior management, and as he held out his hand and introduced himself my impression was of a slouching, mumbling Marlon Brando type character. His name was Rupert Beard and I got the feeling that he either wasn't the world's best communicator or that he didn't suffer fools gladly and everyone else was a fool. "I'll take you over to the lab" he grunted and I followed him the short way across the yard into the factory. This was the main employees' entrance with rows of clocks and clocking in cards and as we passed through and entered the factory proper I was aware of the clattering of cans from overhead tram-like rails as they travelled to some obvious destination. There was the feel of steam heat from huge engine like machines which I was later to discover were called blanchers. We turned left and entered the first door. This was the lab but it was unlike any laboratory I had ever seen, It was a series of three rooms. The first was more like a storeroom with stools, benches, cupboards and a huge chest freezer. We passed through to the lab proper, a bigger room with benches on either side, sinks, scales, test-tubes, strange looking machines and stools on either side. The end room was an office and as we entered the lab a man rose from his desk to meet us. He was in his mid forties, ruddy complexion, but a kindly face. He too wore a white coat which was open down the front and beneath he wore a check shirt and khaki trousers. On his head he wore a green peaked cap, not white, another sign of seniority. His name was Jim Toshak. We were introduced and shook hands. "Let's go in the office" the manager said and we three entered. The door was shut, and the interview began.

There were a few preliminary questions about my previous employment history but that had already been stated on my C.V. and they weren't dwelt on. Then the job description was explained. This was left to Jim. I warmed to this man. His enthusiasm and knowledge came over as he spoke and it was clear he loved his job. The actual job description was 'Process and Quality Controller'. He explained that his department had sole control over all the processing machines in the factory: the blanchers, retorts, exhausters, cookers etc. If he said 'Stop' they stopped and would not start again until he said so. At present there were only two people with this authority in the department, himself, in charge, and Steve Henderson who held a similar position to that which I would hold if I got the job. It would be on the spot training but my authority would start from the outset. Jim was very proud of his position and glancing at Rupert Beard who had sat there passively during this induction he added that he was directly responsible to him as factory manager.

I was already excited about the job and was desperate to make a good impression. But then the blow came. We went to the room with the chest freezer and Jim lifted the lid to show me the range of products they processed. "Of course" he said "It's important that you're not colour blind. You must be able to tell one product from another in their frozen state".

"*Damn!*" Was this to be my Achille's Heel? I had discovered my colour defect when I had tried to join the Fleet Air Arm a few years back, one of many attempts to find my niche in life. They had sent me for what is called the lantern test. You sit in a dark room and respond to coloured lights. Well I didn't, at least not good enough: I failed. Apparently they use coloured bats to wave aircraft down onto ships and recognition is rather crucial. Aircraft carriers are rather expensive. Having said that, I recognise all the primary colours, have no difficulty with traffic lights but am bothered with shades of colour, not colour itself and I hurriedly defended myself. "I have a little problem with shades" I said pointing at bags of frozen produce but I can see easily that they are sprouts and they're strawberries and those are peas and those are blackcurrants. I particularly chose foods of the same size and shape to prove my point. To which Jim said surprisingly "I know what you mean. I'm a bit like that myself". And I breathed inwardly a sigh of relief. I wasn't to know that I would be caught out sometime in the future. Above all, he said, the job involved common sense, integrity, and honesty. I reckoned I scored pretty high on all points. With a final question from Rupert "Do you think you can do the job?" and a resounding "Most definitely" from me, the interview came to an end and a tour of the factory was suggested. I was fitted with a white coat and hat and Rupert took his leave saying they had others to see and I would hear from them soon.

Outside the lab there were several working areas. Huge steam blanchers with metal conveyor belts churned out blanched vegetables of a cabbage looking leaf and women sat at another belt sorting through them as they came their way. Jim said it was curly kale, a winter green, being packed for a shipping line. Other belts stood idle and he explained that they were between seasons and their busy time started in June with the peas. Then they worked seven days a week, twenty four hour a day, through to October. That's why they had to increase their staff. There were several packing areas where boxes were stapled together ready to be filled with produce then deposited into the enormous factory-size deep freeze. Access to this was gained by just pulling on a rope, so sited that fork lift riders didn't need to get down from their vehicles as they entered and left. Then the huge doors slid open and the frosted air crept out. Another rope hung inside to close them. We entered and I felt the chill immediately. The workers inside wore thick Eskimo-like duffel coats and hoods and you could hear the whine of the trucks as they lifted pallets onto huge stacks from floor to ceiling. We were not dressed for this climate and I wasn't sorry when we emerged. As we did the chilly March day suddenly felt very warm.

"We draw our own water from bore wells." Jim said "and we have our own sewage farm so we're pretty self sufficient. All of these things come under our jurisdiction." Finally we entered the stores, the dry stores that is, for as well as freezing, fruit and veg. were canned. There is a saying in the industry 'Freeze what you can- and can what you can't.' From these stores came all the boxes and cans and all the filled cans were returned and stored here.

By now I was already won over and whether or not my excitement showed I knew that being unsuccessful in gaining the job would be a major disappointment. The tour finished outside the factory office and Jim said he hoped I'd enjoyed my visit and they would be in touch in a couple of days and we shook hands. "Thank you Mr.Toshak" I said politely "You've been very helpful. I've really enjoyed it."

"Everybody calls me Tosh" he replied, smiling "We're on first name terms here" which had a certain irony as it was his surname but I knew what he meant and he turned and left. I also turned and headed off to the station to find out when the next train was due back to Norwich. As I did the dreaded thought came to me that tomorrow I would be back in the clutches of Miss Belsham.

Chapter 2

One month later I arrived to begin my new career. The letter had come, two days later as promised, offering me the job and my life had changed. I couldn't contain the joy as I gave in my notice at the tax office, the statutory one month, and the last few weeks I actually enjoyed the work. It was customary when talking to a defaulter to make a note on their file to chase them up in a month's time if they still hadn't coughed up with the cash and as I did so each time I thought *"But it won't be me-hooray!"*

I presented myself at the lab which was a hive of industry. Two women, in white overalls and headscarves, were busy at one of the benches with their hands in something messy. Another man, taller and broader than me with white coat and green hat was talking to Tosh in his office. On seeing me Tosh rose with a smile and said "John! Welcome to Westwick! Everyone! This is John. I've told you about him. He's come to join the happy band."

"For his sins" interjected the other man and they all laughed. "This is Steve" said Tosh indicating the speaker. You'll be working with him for a while till you learn the ropes. We shook hands. He seemed an amiable sort of chap and as time went on I never had recourse to change my initial opinion of him. Bringing me to the two women sitting there, who had stopped working to join in the introductions, he introduced us. "These two ladies are the backbone of the establishment" They made various comments, like they felt a pay-rise was coming, and he continued "This is May and this is Phyllis. Anything you want, if I, or Steve aren't here, just ask them." We shook hands. May was the older of the two, around fifty, short, a little plump with a kindly face. Phyllis wore spectacles, was younger, probably mid-thirties, slimmer with a more questioning face, and as I was to discover later, quite outspoken. "First things first ladies we'd better get him kitted out. Steve show him where to put his things and we'll find something to fit him." I followed Steve to the first of the three rooms which afforded some privacy because it was the only room that didn't have a window overlooking the factory. There was where you hung your coat, ate your lunch or enjoyed some respite from the demands on you. The ladies brought an assortment of coats and hats for me to try on and soon I was proudly adorned in a size that fitted. I must say that I'm really not a hat person and very proud of my well quiffed hairstyle but well ' needs must' and I only had to wear it everytime I entered the factory, which turned out to be in the next few seconds, for at that moment a woman charge-hand appeared at the door and requested the number one blancher be turned on. "Okay Christine" replied Tosh and she left. "Steve ! You do it, and take John with you. Let him see what happens."

"Right!" replied Steve and we got up and went out.

For Steve it was an everyday occurrence. This was what the job was all about; starting up, closing down, setting temperatures, monitoring temperatures and he didn't have to think about it, but for me this was the beginning of a whole new world and as we walked across the factory floor it seemed as if the whole world was watching me. To say the least I was intimidated by the rows of women sitting at the conveyor belt waiting for something to do. That was why we were there but I was also aware that my white coat looked clean and new whilst others looked lived in. Christine, the charge-hand was waiting. She was very tall, at least six feet. I'm five feet eight and I felt short beside her. She was a well built lady, yet slim, and not at first sight attractive until she smiled and spoke and I was aware that she and Steve had a certain rapport between them. Steve introduced me to her and she smiled and said hello. There was a bit of jovial banter between them about 'not going to learn much from him' and she left to deal with something or other whilst Steve explained the procedure. The blancher is a huge open-topped machine through which produce is passed on a metal conveyor whilst being bombarded by either hot water or steam. It's not a cooker but it's purpose is to kill enzymes in the material which might otherwise reduce the shelf life when in storage. The food item today was mushrooms. A whole pallet stood waiting at the end of the blancher for it to be switched on. On the side of it were various valves and Steve began to turn them on allowing jets of steam onto the belt, then he started the blancher up and the whole thing thundered into life. He gave the okay to Christine and she instructed workers to feed the mushrooms onto the elevator which fed the blancher. This was the chain of command which I was to learn and adopt. Steve pointed out the two crucial factors in blanching, one the amount of heat and the other the length of time under the heat – i.e. the speed of the belt. At the end of the blancher, cold water was sprayed on the mushrooms to cool them down so the women waiting could handle them. After two minutes or so they cascaded onto the belt and the women picked over them, removing anything foreign or unsightly. We walked along the lines and Steve chatted away at familiar faces. I was introduced to those who cared to ask who I was and everyone seemed friendly. Most of the women were mid to old married women. There were some younger girls but they were usually put to the heavier jobs or those that required them to be on their feet for a while. After a few minutes Steve climbed up onto the side of the blancher and picked one or two hot mushrooms. "Be careful" he said "When you climb up here make sure you know which pipes to hold onto. Some off them are jolly hot." He jumped down "Here-try one" he said and offered me a button mushroom which was still hot. I have to admit that this was my first taste of mushroom of any kind and I tentatively bit into it. I wasn't that impressed but I tried not to be too derogatory. "It's an acquired taste" he said "I love them. Now I'll show you what we do with these" showing me those he had in his hand. I followed him back to the lab where he proceeded to show me how they tested whether they had got the temperature right. He cut the mushroom in half down through the stalk, poured a mixture of hydrogen peroxide and something called guaiacol into a petri-dish and placed the cut mushroom in it, cut side down. Then depending on the colour change to the cut surface he could judge if he'd got the blanching time right. This time he had. I was most impressed. Tosh came over. "We do this with all veg as well, but things as small as peas we mince first and put in a test tube" Just then another head appeared at the door with a problem and Steve went off to attend to it. Tosh took me to one side to explain what I might expect to happen over the months ahead. "A lot of what we freeze during the summer is brought out in the winter to can. This enables us to keep our regular staff busy. The seasonal staff arrive next month, then we are really busy. When you are confident to make decisions on your own I must impress on you the importance of honesty, by that I mean if you make a mistake you must admit to it. That way we can put it right. No one will blame you but if you try to cover mistakes up it could cause the company dearly, plus we are dealing with food and therefore people's health. We mustn't take risks. If you don't understand anything always ask. Okay?" I agreed and hoped that my mistakes wouldn't be disastrous ones.

May and Phyllis it turned out were on permanent secondment to the lab from the factory floor and were part of the furniture. Their duties were several and varied, including looking after us, seeing to the laundry, washing used instruments and preparing samples of excellence to send to prospective customers. Our store cupboards were full of perfect sample cans of fruit and veg. which could be sent out if requested, but were also used to replace those that customers had complained about. Usually two or three good ones were sent as compensation for one which might not have come up to standard for a variety of reasons i.e. a daisy head in a can of peas or too many misshapen berries in a can of strawberries. Preparing these perfect replacements was to be one of the tasks I was to become proficient in. During the rest of my first day I watched, learned, accompanied and marvelled at the variety of things the job entailed and at the end of the day I admit to being exhausted and filled with so much information that I fell asleep on the train and didn't wake up till it pulled into Thorpe Station, my destination in Norwich.

Over the next few days and weeks I was instructed in all the facets of our responsibility, but still accompanied Tosh or Steve when an actual function needed doing or a decision needed making. I learnt the names of people and felt at home as the newness of the situation wore off. When I had no specific task to do I was encouraged to wander about the factory to see how things worked, where things went etc. It was important that I knew the factory inside out, for after all it was the essence of the job that all production was supervised. I should mention at this stage that we had no power over staff whatsoever. If we saw things weren't right we told those wearing green hats, the supervisors, and they dealt with it. There was of course a hierarchy here too. Opposite the laboratory, the other side of the canning line, was the staff supervisors' office. It was simply a glass building so they could see out over the factory. There were two senior managers to cover different shifts, Bill Thompson and Peter Norton. Bill did everything according to the book which is not a criticism but it made him less approachable than Peter who was always cracking jokes and was subsequently easier to talk to. Others I got to know were Horace the syrup man who made the syrups and brines for the canned goods. His room was next door to the staff office and was full of vats, sacks and a variety of colouring agents .He was a jolly man that nothing could faze. Then there was Ernie the mechanic who looked after the working of the canning line, an able yet obliging man that everybody liked. Bert the boiler man was based next to the lab in the boiler house. He was, again, a friendly man near to retirement and was responsible for the steam which fed the blanchers, retorts, canning lines and steam hoses which were essential for cleaning down the machines at the end of shifts. Then there was Jimmy. He was always around, pushing trolleys, shunting loads from one place to another. Nothing was too much trouble for him. He never grumbled and was always cheerful, cracking jokes with the ladies and generally bringing a smile to those with whom he worked. True, he was put upon because of his good nature but he always remained cheerful.

Of course I also learnt the names of some of the girls who were my age or younger and who worked in the various departments. Two of them in particular were sisters, Josie the eldest was 18 and Melanie the youngest 16. Both were extremely attractive, though white wrap- around overalls and headscarves were not the most flattering clothes to wear, even so I found myself noticing them more and more. There were others too, brash and forward who were ready to pull my leg whenever possible. Some of them I gave a wide berth, but it was all in good fun and I enjoyed each day as it came.

The canteen was over by the office block and that was a good place to meet people. Tosh brought his own sandwiches which he ate in his office, often with his feet up on the desk but even lunch time wasn't sacrosanct as we could be called out at any time. Steve also brought his own lunch most of the time and sat at what became our end of the lab, the store room. I did the same out of necessity to cut the cost. I had travelling expenses and train fares weren't cheap. I was earning around £11 a week and was on a salary. This meant that we didn't clock in, which was good, but it also meant we couldn't improve our wages with overtime. So I decided to invest in a moped type bike. It was called an N.S.U. Quickly. It wasn't new. It had been a demonstration model for a distributor and like our special cans of fruit or veg it had been made to a high standard so as to impress purchasers. It also had a pillion seat so I could take a passenger if required, and time would show it came in very handy. This gave me more freedom as I was no longer tied to train times, which was even more beneficial when I started doing irregular hours. Tosh could drive but didn't have a car though he had access to company vehicles when he needed them. He preferred to cycle to work from his home the other side of Worstead, a little place called Dilham. His garden was his pride and joy along with his family. He had several daughters and a son. Steve lived in Hoveton Near Wroxham on the Broads and came to work on a motor-bike. He was a single

Frozen In Time

man, two or three years my senior, who enjoyed his work and seemed to enjoy life in general. He would often be seen still chatting away long after his shift had finished. He was very popular with everyone in the factory especially the ladies. I was just happy to be a member of this team.

Chapter 3

April passed quickly into May and more and more crops were being harvested and brought into the factory. One of the first was rhubarb. This was brought in, minus the leaves, topped and tailed, then the stalks were laid on a conveyor belt which took them speedily through a series of circular blades so spaced that pieces of fruit came out all about an inch long, ideal for frozen packs or to be put in cans. I noticed that Josie was among the girls feeding the rhubarb in. I observed for a while then had to return to something in the lab. Sometime later someone burst into the lab in an obvious panic and shouted that a girl had had an accident on the rhubarb cutter and there was blood everywhere. We all dashed out. There was turmoil at the scene. Charge -hands were attending a girl lying on the floor and they were surrounded by women uttering all manner of expressions of horror. I hurried to see who the girl was and I admit to a feeling of relief when I saw it wasn't Josie and as I looked up I saw her amongst the crowd which was now being kept back by one of the supervisors. Our eyes met and she managed a frightened smile to which I smiled back with what I hoped was understanding and some comfort.

    It turned out that the girl in question had broken one of the cardinal rules of the job. Whenever something jams up in a machine it must be switched off, the guard removed and the obstruction cleared. She had, however, attempted to push the sticks through with her hand, beyond the safety cover, result, the loss of the tip of her finger. She was taken to the nurse in the first aid room and subsequently to hospital whilst we were left to clear up the mess and the women were given another task. Needless to say we didn't find the bit of finger and a lot of rhubarb was wasted that day, and I had experienced a feeling inside me towards Josie that was both unsettling and yet rather pleasant.

Frozen In Time

Of all the jobs in the factory, the one I never liked, was to do with the pump house. Set off to the right of the site was the brick building that housed the three pumps that drew the water from the bore wells. Beside them was a huge galvanised tank which held a soda solution. Soda and chlorine both had to be filtered into the water system, soda from the tank and chlorine from huge, pressurised canisters. The soda was poured into the tanks from sacks and from the outset I developed a sneezing allergy to the powder as it came out of the sacks. I would sneeze and sneeze till my eyes watered and I'd have to leave the room till the dust settled, then go back in to stir up the solution which still affected me though not quite as badly. Dealing with the chlorine was my biggest fear. Chlorine is a heavy, poisonous, deadly gas and the cylinders were connected to the pipes that fed the factory. Every so often however the cylinders needed changing. There was a safety procedure for this. A large metal key turned off the cylinder from the top so it could be removed, but then the problem came. The new cylinder had to be manhandled outside and they were too heavy to carry. The only way was to sort of wiggle-walk them. Standing them outside it was wise to point the nozzle in the opposite direction to the prevailing wind, if indeed there was a wind, then with the key give a quick turn to open the valve then shut it immediately and move away quickly upwind. Although this sounds a bit like Russian Roulette there was a purpose to it. The valves tend to get dirt in them when standing around and by blowing them off you save the problem of blocked pipes later on. It was not a job I cherished. I had this fear that I would open the valve alright, and they were very tight, but not be able to close it, or I would drop the key after opening it, and bending down to retrieve it come into contact with the gas, which being heavy falls to the ground, and I would never get up again. Worse still the cylinder would continue to spurt out its deadly gas to affect the whole factory- a major catastrophe. Obviously this never happened, and usually two of us would do it together, but I always feared it would require attention when I was on my own. Outside the lab was a huge bell which was connected to the pumps. This was there to tell us if the pumps suddenly stopped. They were very vulnerable to power surges. My first experience of it came during a particularly bad storm with lightning. The bell suddenly started ringing, an enormous volume of noise which could be heard over all the factory noise. Nobody had told me about it and Steve was out of the lab so quick and heading for the exit that I wondered whatever had happened. Tosh explained that lightning can trip the switch and we have to get there fast and press the restart button to get them going again, otherwise, if left, they could be a hell of a job to get started again. Just another job that fell to us.

Other crops that appeared during May were turnip tops. That is those grown for the fresh young leaves and harvested before the turnips developed. These were blanched and packed in what were called catering packs and sold to shipping lines as young greens.

Gooseberries appeared at the end of May, beginning of June, and were either frozen or canned. For those of you who have ever had the task of topping and tailing gooseberries by hand, there is an easy way. Place them in a carborundum drum, that is one with an abrasive surface inside, then spin the drum round fast and as the fruit is bounced about inside, all protrusions are removed. This also has the advantage of breaking the waterproof skin of the gooseberry therefore allowing it to better absorb the syrup when canned.

And canned they were in their thousands. The canning line came alive. I never ceased to be amazed by this operation. If you have ever been fascinated by toy trains and railway tracks, well this was a big boy's toy. The cans started their journey from the stores across the yard. They rose up elevators, then across the yard on tracks pushed by their own momentum, then down into the factory, twisting and turning cleverly so they ended up the right way, that is, open end up. Yes they did jam up sometimes and start bombarding anyone beneath but toy trains get derailed too. Don't they? When they reach their destination they get filled with fruit, then syrup, piped from the syrup room and they continue through an open topped tank of very hot water called an exhauster. Here they travel back and forth on underwater tracks, till any trapped air is exhausted out. Then the lids are put on by a seaming machine and the cans are ready for cooking.

My involvement was with the exhauster. It had to be a certain temperature to expand the contents, then when they were cooked and cooled they would contract, thus creating a vacuum, and as nature abhors a vacuum so any harmful microbes couldn't survive. To monitor the temperature we had circular charts which were clock–timed and the temperature was recorded by a fine ink pen in graph form, hence the need for constant vigilance. Many familiar faces were working on this line including Josie, and Jimmy was there as usual putting everybody in a good mood with his jokes. I had started them up, having checked with Ernie that the seam on the lids would be of the right size. It always was. He was a man you could trust, and away they went. Shortly after Phyllis came out of the lab to tell me something and while I listened I caught Josie looking across at us. Once again she smiled and Phyllis noticed. "That girl's got 'come to bed' eyes" she said and disappeared into the lab. I'd never heard that expression before, having lived quite a sheltered life with a chapel background and I wondered *"Has she? Does she look at everyone like that? Or is it just me?"* I hoped it was the latter but for a day or two I paid particular attention to girls' eyes. I wasn't sure what I was looking for, but after a couple of days I knew. Not all girls had them, but Josie certainly did. I managed to glean from the other girls that Josie's sister Melanie had a boyfriend but Josie hadn't, which I found strange for such an attractive girl with such promise in her eyes, strange but also encouraging.

It was during these canning runs that Tosh's warning about honesty was to be tested. Because the floor of the factory was always wet or littered with vegetation we had to wear rubber boots all the time which was not the best footwear for the health of our feet but was certainly practical and large rubber gloves were also at our disposal when handling hot cans. Every so often I would don the gloves and lift a can from the exhauster and test the temperature in the middle of the can. Then I could adjust the amount of heat the exhauster needed. On returning later from other duties I glanced at the temperature graph only to find that the temperature had dropped quite drastically from the required 175f to 160f. I immediately called a halt. All switches went up, all stop buttons got pressed. The line came to a standstill. Everybody looked. The charge-hand came over "*What do I do now?*" I wondered. Fortunately Tosh had heard the sudden silence and appeared on the scene. I explained what had happened and he said "Well done John" and proceeded to show me how to isolate those cans which had just passed through. "They'll be placed on one side in the stores and we'll test them later to make sure they're alright, but you did exactly right –well done!" We brought the exhauster up to temperature and away we went again. His praise had made me feel accepted, a real member of the team. My confidence was growing.

To understand how my first physical contact with Josie came about I must explain how produce was frozen at this time. After being looked over by the women on the inspection belts the food was laid out on metal trays. These trays were then slid onto trolleys which held about 20 trays. They were then wheeled to a chiller room which was the ante room to the freezer itself. Eventually they were shunted into the freezer where they stayed for the required freezing time. The freezer was a tunnel and they came out at the other end. The trolleys were pulled out, the trays emptied and the food packed. It was at the exit that the need for gloves was obligatory. If frozen metal comes into contact with skin the skin will stick to it. Any attempt to pull yourself free results in freezer burns which are extremely painful. It was whilst on my rounds that Josie and her associates had just arrived to deal with the frozen trays. I don't know how it happened and I hold some responsibility for distracting her but whilst the girls were doing their usual mickey taking, Josie, forgetting to put on her gloves, grabbed hold of the top tray to remove it. She knew at once her mistake as her fingers were stuck to the tray. She cried out, not in pain, but from the cold and the realisation of the situation. Immediately I told her not to pull away. I thought briefly then had an idea. The syrup room was a few feet away. "Don't move!" I said and disappeared. The syrup room had plenty of warm water and grabbing a jug I filled it and hurried back to Josie. She was getting a little panicky and lots of advice from the other girls but she was still attached to the tray. Quickly I poured the water directly onto the point of contact and to our relief it thawed sufficiently for her to remove her hands. I put down the jug and said "Let me see" and held both hands to check she wasn't burned. "They look alright" I said "Are you sure you're alright?"

" Yes" she replied "Thanks to you."

"As long as you're sure" I said "Perhaps you should see the nurse."

"No really" she insisted. Then she gave a coy smile and said "Why don't you kiss them better?" to which all of the girls burst into laughter. But I was up to the challenge and not to be outdone, I lifted each hand in turn and kissed her finger tips and as my head came up, now so much nearer to her face I was again mesmerised by her deep blue, enchanting eyes. I felt bewitched and under her spell, but that spell was soon broken by Christine the charge hand entering the room and telling the girls to get a move on. Then with a twinkle in her eye she told me in no uncertain terms to clear off and leave her girls alone. I picked up the jug and made my way promptly.

It was hard to concentrate for the rest of the day but I got through it with no misadventures. I was of course still on a sort of probation and couldn't afford to make mistakes. Five o' clock was my usual leaving off time. It was also the end of the day shift. The night cleaning staff took over then and there was a flurry of people clocking off and heading for home. I left shortly after and headed for the cycle sheds where my moped was kept. Most of the cars and bikes had left but I noticed someone with a bike who seemed in no hurry to leave. As I got closer I realised it was Josie. In the factory everybody dresses alike so out of work it's sometimes hard to recognise people. Now that she wasn't hidden in a headscarf I noticed her long, naturally wavy, fair hair which framed her face perfectly. If I thought she was attractive before, she looked stunning now.

"Hello" I said "Not in trouble again I hope."

"No" she smiled "I just wanted to see you to thank you properly for helping me this morning."

"It was nothing" I said "It was probably my fault for distracting you."

" No. I should have known better. Thanks anyway."

"Well if you ever find yourself stuck with a problem, let me know."

"I'll remember that" she said laughing.

" Do you live far?" I asked, desperate to prolong the conversation.

"No. Only about a couple of miles. It isn't far."

"Doesn't your sister travel with you?"

"Usually but she wasn't well today."

"Oh, sorry to hear that. Nothing serious I hope?"

She hesitated, then said "No, not really" For a moment there was an awkward pause, neither of us knowing what to say next, then she said "Are you going to the fete on Saturday?"

"Which one is that ?" I asked.

"There's one on at Worstead, in the afternoon-2pm"

"Are you going?" I said.

"Probably. There isn't much happens round here at weekends."

"Well I might come then," I said as she began to wheel her bike out of the shed.

"I'd better be off now, bye then" and she pushed on the pedals and started to move away.

"Goodbye Josie" I said and she turned at the sound of her name, smiled and continued up the drive. It was the first time I had used her name and it felt good. Had I said '*I might come*

Frozen In Time

then'? Who was I kidding? I knew damn well I was going. I couldn't wait.

Chapter 4

The fete was nothing out of the ordinary, a typical Summer affair, though strictly speaking it was still Spring. We were still at the end of May. It was a lovely sunny day and people from all around had arrived to a field just off the main village square. It also incorporated a dog show and though I am not overly fond of dogs I can appreciate that others are. The fete was to be opened by Pete Murray, a well-known disc jockey on the radio and t.v. and no doubt that had attracted many there. But for me the attraction was a 5foot 2 inches, slim, attractive, fair-haired girl with blue eyes, and after parking my bike in a nearby barn that a local farmer had made available I set off on my search. 'Beatles' music was playing over the loudspeakers and I wandered amongst the usual array of stalls. There were games to play, plant stalls, home-made produce to buy and a large marquee where refreshments could be had and it wasn't long before I began to recognise people I knew from the factory. Everybody was milling about in the warm sunshine, which had brought out more Summer clothes than had been seen lately. I had arrived as near as possible to 2pm. and the loudspeaker interrupted the music to welcome everybody and announce the presence of the guest of honour Pete Murray. He then gave a short speech, pleaded with us to spend a lot of money as the fete was for the church then disappeared with some dignitaries towards the beer tent. I remembered thinking "*I wonder how much he gets paid for that?*".

My search for Josie proved fruitless, though if I'd seen her I didn't know what I'd say to her. After all we didn't have a date or anything. I had no claim to her and for all I know it was just her being friendly. The dog show was just about to start in a ring marked out by rope and surrounded by straw bales. I got myself a drink and sat on one of the bales. Five or ten minutes later the dogs started their parade prior to them doing clever tricks through hoops, up slides and over fences. I class dog shows with jugglers and acrobats: very clever but not particularly entertaining, although I think dog shows have the edge, especially when they ignore their owners and do their own thing.

After sitting for a while I was aware on the other side of the ring a group of lads and girls laughing and playing around together and my heart leapt as I recognised Josie as one of them. She was dressed in a long blue dress with a white collar and matching white belt and she was chatting happily to two of the lads. They were teasing her and she appeared to be taunting them, and all of a sudden I felt out of place. I was in turmoil. I wanted to stay and I wanted to go and I might have gone then but for the arrival of two of the girls who I had often seen with Josie at the factory who came and sat on the next bale. They recognised me immediately and said hello. Their names were Wendy and June and they were both eating icecreams. "Are you on your own?" asked Wendy.

"Yes" I replied "I thought I'd come and see what's going on."

"And have you?" asked June taking an enormous lick of her icecream.

"What?"

"Seen what's going on?"

"Oh yes-I think so."

" It's good isn't it?"

"What is?"

"The fete of course. What did you think I meant?"

"Oh! Yes it's great but I 'm not staying I've seen most of it." and with that I got up, said goodbye and ambled off. I had made up my mind to go, and meandered amongst the stalls towards the parking area. It took me a little while. I was waylaid by a lady running the tombola who persuaded me to buy a ticket. I bought two but in keeping with the day so far I was out of luck. I arrived at the barn to pick up my bike and was just about to put on my helmet when I heard a voice I recognised, I turned and it was Josie.

"Wendy told me you were here."
"Oh-right" I said weakly.
"Are you going?" she said.
"Well – yes. I thought I would."
"But you never said hello."
"No."
"Why not?"
"Well I-I thought you were busy. I didn't want to interrupt."
"Interrupt what?"
"You were with company. I didn't want to gatecrash."
"But I wanted you to come."
"Did you? I wasn't sure."
"I looked forward to it."
"So did I."
"Then don't go."
"But what about your friends?"
"Which friends?"
"The boys you were with."
"Oh them, they're just boys from the village." then she hesitated "Is that why you're leaving? because of them?"
"No!-well partly."
"Oh you are silly" She walked towards me.
"Well I'm not perfect" She was close enough to me now that I could smell her perfume.
"I think you're rather sweet."
"Am I ? Is that good or bad?"
"It depends on what you think of me" Now she was right in front of me looking up and I gazed into her eyes "I think you're lovely" I said.
"That's alright then" she almost whispered. I don't know who kissed who. We were on a collision course and it was the most delicious feeling of warmth and tenderness I had ever felt. I could feel her breasts lightly against my chest and I would have prolonged this moment forever but she pulled away, took my hand in hers and said "Now you're staying. Come on" and led me back to the fete. We spent the rest of the

afternoon together enjoying the entertainment provided. Even my luck changed on the tombola and I won a bottle of lemonade which we both shared. Suddenly this 'nothing out of the ordinary' fete in a Norfolk field was the most wonderful place on earth.

We met Melanie, Josie's sister who was with her boyfriend. He was a man called Tom, about 25 or 6 I judged, a rather surly looking farmhand and I didn't take to him at all. I wondered what such an attractive girl as Melanie could see in someone like that. Christine, the charge hand, was there too, looking quite different out of her restricting work's uniform and showing a well developed figure in skirt and blouse. She also noticed us and smiling said something about 'still bothering her girls'.

The afternoon passed far too quickly and people began drifting home. Josie lived in Upper Street, Sloley, the next village south of Worstead and I offered to give her a lift. She was reluctant at first as she'd come with some friends but said if she let them know it would be all right. Five minutes later we were getting ready to go. I had a jacket so I gave her my coat to wear, and my helmet. She wasn't really dressed for speed riding. Not that I drove very fast. I wasn't sure where to go and the feel of her arms around me as she hung on was a feeling I didn't want to end too soon. She directed me along the country roads which only took a few minutes and she told me to stop just before a row of cottages. She didn't want to stop right outside her house so she got off and I took back my coat and helmet.

"It's been a lovely afternoon" I said.
"I've enjoyed it too. I'm glad you came."
"So am I."
"You going home now?"
"Yes. Fraid so. Which road do I take to get me back on the Coltishall Rd.?"

She pointed the way, through the village, turn right for Scottow and straight on. Glancing at the row of cottages I asked which was hers.

"The third" she replied "I'd better go in." Then she came to me. I put my arm round her slim waist and we kissed. "See you on Monday" I whispered and she said good bye and walked away. I watched her all the way till she reached the door. She turned, gave me a little wave, and went in. I put on my coat and helmet and drove away. For me, Monday couldn't come too soon.

Chapter 5

Flaming June, and it was too. The warm weather had brought the peas to an early maturity. The work force had doubled, plus there was a contingent of Irish students who were billeted in a couple of huge Nissan huts at the end of the site. Basic bed and blankets were provided all for ten shillings a week and the students were deployed all over the factory.

My relationship with Josie blossomed, though time was soon to be restricted. Steve was on nights which didn't bother him whilst Tosh and I were left to cope with the days. I had met Josie after work most days and had seen her the occasional evening, choosing not to go home till very late. But all that was to change as my shift was extended from 9 to 12 hours which meant I didn't finish till 8pm, and furthermore we now began to work weekends as well. Still we had some time together at lunch break and I saw her briefly before she went home. Buses were laid on to bring people from the neighbouring villages and she took advantage of them.

The pea harvest waited for nobody. It was all controlled by the Field Office. That was a group of men with agriculural know-how who tested the peas for their optimum time of harvesting. Then the countryside came alive with huge viners descending on the fields where the peas were dredged from the ground, vined and shelled and the peas poured into huge hoppers in their millions. Even at night with lights flashing, like alien spaceships, they continued to whine and vine regardless of anyone unfortunate enough to live nearby and trying to get some sleep. Then the hoppers were brought to the factory. Peas in their fresh vined state smell and taste delicious but there is only so long, heaped in hoppers, that they can stay like this. We reckoned two hours, then they began to sweat and had to be blanched. Every blancher in the factory was in full use and they poured in and out endlessly. Women were on every inspection line picking out foreign bodies, pods that had slipped through, daisy heads and anything else unwanted and the peas poured off the end of the belt like lemmings falling off a cliff to their death. This was where the students came in, lifting the trays and packing them on trolleys for freezing. It was back breaking work but they needed the work to fund their education in Ireland and the wages were much higher here than back home. Some of them would work two shifts at a time, upto 24 hours before collapsing on their beds exhausted. I even met one who claimed to have worked 40 hours with just tea breaks. I think the factory act would have had something to say about that.

When you harvest a whole field of peas you get the whole range from mature to immature peas and these had to be graded. This was done in a remarkably clever, yet simple way. From the blancher the peas fell into a circular vat through which water flowed in a spiral of channels. This water was a special brine solution, which had the effect of altering the density of the water. As a result the heavier peas sank to the bottom and were fed off onto one belt whilst the younger, sweeter peas tended to float and were fed off on another belt entirely. Thus we were able to grade them with such names as 'Special', 'Fine Standard', and 'Good Value'. But even this required constant checking and this was how I became a pea taster. Tosh was the expert at this. He had been tasting peas for years and knew one grade from another. Steve had also learnt and I was in training. It simply required taking a handful of peas from the belt and chewing them, but not so simple was deciding what to call them and I was given lots of initiating in the different tastes until I could make a reasonable judgement. I always felt a bit of a fraud at this because there were many people there who had worked here for years and probably could do it better, but someone had to make these decisions and it was down to us.

June was also the month for strawberries, and many farms were down to contract with us to provide them. Down towards the railway line was the sewage farm. Water was essential for

Frozen In Time

our work and disposal was equally important. Lennie the sewage man lived there, in his office come pump house. He was a man from another age, dressed in a blue boiler suit with a blue peaked cap looking just as I imagined train drivers to look. He had old fashioned ideas about many things and I remember him saying that toilets had no place in a home. He wouldn't have one in his and they belonged in a yard. But not every thing about him was antiquated as the pin-ups in his office showed. They were the next stage up from National Geographical Magazine for sex education. As the strawberries came onto flower there was always the danger of late frosts, so pipes from the sewage farm were laid to the strawberry fields with sprays attached. If frost was imminent a thermometer triggered a bell in the pumphouse and also, so I believe, in Lennie's home. it was then upto him to get to the factory and proceed to pump the water to the strawberry fields. By coating the flowers with water it protected them from the frost, thus saving the crop. Unfortunately for him this usually happened at night. Incidentally, if you were wondering, this wasn't sewage from the toilets but from the washing down of factory floors, and each day we had to chlorinate and test the water for it's purity. Surplus water was also pumped to fields near the factory where osiers were grown, that is willow stems which are used in all manner of horticulture for fences, basket making etc. They needed an unlimited supply of water to grow well.

By now, Josie and I ,were common knowledge and though I'd preferred it not to be so widespread it couldn't be avoided. Whenever I saw her during the day, working somewhere or other there would be the usual ribbing like "He's checking up on you Josie" or from the older women "When you get fed up with him Josie, let me know, I'll have him" In the lab May was encouraging saying "Enjoy yourself lad, life's too short" Whilst Phyllis warned "Watch that girl, she's a flighty one" and Tosh and Steve just stood and grinned. But later on Tosh, who was a bit of a romantic I discovered, took me to one side and said "Just don't let it interfere with your work" I said that it wouldn't, but secretly I thought *'how could it not?'* But I knew what he meant.

Lunchtime gave us a little time together but I tried not to appear too possessive, and besides, lunch was invariably interrupted with a call of one kind or another over the tannoy requiring me somewhere else. In the morning break the usual occupation was the Star newspaper crossword. It was very easy and the challenge was to get it finished in the ten minutes. One of the distractions, over the lunchtime, strangely enough was the game of draughts, something I had long since grown out of and moved on to chess, a much more intellectual and challenging game, but Ernie the mechanic had apparently been draughts champion in the army and had quite a reputation for it. This was not draughts as we played it as children where if you didn't take a piece you were huffed i.e. your piece was taken, no this was highly manipulative draughts, where if you could take a piece you had to, and Ernie was a master at this. He would let you take two or three pieces so you felt really good then he would swoop all over the board removing four of yours all in one go. I had more than one game with him, thinking it couldn't be that hard to beat him but he showed no mercy and left me totally beaten. In all the time I knew him I never knew anyone to get the better of him.

By now I was fully fledged in all the aspects of my job but the beauty of the work was that no two days were alike and you never knew what was going to happen next. There was no time to get bored. True I had to adjust when new crops came in that I'd never confronted before but that was the challenge. Some of these foods were sent from the Chairman of the Company from Westwick Hall for his own use and that of his friends. Peaches, nectarines, apricots were grown in greenhouses at the hall and delivered directly to the lab. It was May and Phyllis's job to look them over and put them in cans. We of course all had to sample them to check they were all right, it was one of the perks of the job. Those that were left were canned personally by us. Outside the lab we had our own canning line, It consisted of a tank of water about three feet square heated by a steam pipe and our own manual canning machine. When the cans were ready, filled with syrup fom the syrup room, we would don the huge rubber gloves and place a tray into the tank. We followed the same procedure as the canning line only nothing moved around. When the cans were upto exhausting temperature, one by one we put the lids on. Then they were put in a small retort in the lab and cooked for the appropriate time then cooled. These cans were then labelled and put in the Chairman's stock. We repeated this procedure with every food item that came into the factory, special samples that we knew were perfect to send out in case of complaints. I really enjoyed this job but it had to be fitted in with the running of the factory.

The days passed with unrelenting pressure. That lovely smell of fresh sweet peas that heralded the beginning of the pea season had now been displaced with a sour, pungent smell that no amount of cleaning could erase. Even though everything was steam cleaned thoroughly between the hours of 6 and 8 a.m. it still somehow managed to pervade the whole factory. I thought I would never eat a meal with peas again and wondered if I would end up feeling like this about all veg.

I really missed seeing Josie for longer periods. That afternoon at the fete will remain with me always but I craved more days like that. She was a young beautiful girl and I was afraid that she might get bored with our long absences and look elsewhere. I longed to take her out, dancing, to the cinema, to the coast, make a day of it, make her feel good, tell her she was lovely,-all those things that young people do together. She had told me that there wasn't much to do in the country and I'd seen the sort of bloke her sister was with. What if someone like that came along and swept her off her feet ? I couldn't bear it. Upto now, outside of work, we had met near to her home and enjoyed walks in the late evening sun. She'd showed me places she'd known all her life as we wandered along hedgerows full of the heady fragrance of cow parsley, around fields full of ripening corn and kissed in the shelter of trees or barns. I'd not yet met her parents and that wasn't high on my agenda, nor it seemed on Josie's. If she wanted me to I would but for now just being with her was all I wanted.

At the end of the month the strawberries arrived, followed two weeks later by raspberries and a few loganberries. They were either frozen or canned and were a pleasant addition to the sandwiches I usually brought for lunch, though whenever the canning line was running we had to take samples after they were cooked, open and check them, and there was nothing to stop us from eating the lot if we so desired, but there is a limit to the amount one could gorge.

It was about now that I became aware that I hadn't seen Josie's sister Melanie for quite some time and I asked Josie if she'd left and got a job somewhere else. After looking around to see that we weren't overheard she said "She's pregnant".

"Oh really" I said, not knowing what one should say in these situations. Then I added "Is she pleased?"

"It's a bit difficult."

"How do you mean?"

"Well it wasn't planned. Mum's furious about it."

"I see" Well I didn't really but I had to say something. "What about her boyfriend Tom, is he sticking by her?"

"That's what mum's mad about. She doesn't think he's good enough for her. She'd wanted someone better for her."

"And what about you?"

"Oh I think she could do better……"

"No. I meant what does she want for you?"

"What all mothers want I suppose, to see their daughters married and well cared for."

"And your father?"

"Oh he wants what mum wants. Anything to keep the peace."

Chapter 6

The normal season for the peas is about six weeks. Those that can't be harvested in time are left to grow on to maturity and then harvested later on for next year's seed, so the farmer doesn't miss out. There were various varieties; Kelvedon Wonder, Onward, Meteor, each harvested in their own time to give succession, and in the lab we had an ingenious machine to test their maturity. It was called a Maturometer. It consisted of a square plate in which were drilled about a hundred holes in which peas could be placed and not fall through. Above each hole was a steel rod. The idea was that the rods would descend on a motor, all at the same time, and pierce the peas and the resistance put up by the peas, which depended on their maturity, would be registered on a needled gauge. What was also clever was that a car windscreen, wiper motor had been adapted so that after coming down, the metal spikes rose back up again just as wipers on a car go back and forth, very ingenious.This latter idea was, I believe, patented here at Westwick. The biggest draw back was placing a hundred peas on a metal plate each time, and of course the washing up afterwards. There was another larger machine called a Tenderometer which did a similar thing, but you just put a handful of peas in and they got crushed, much easier.

    The students came and went, though some stayed the course. We had a couple under our jurisdiction. Their job was to sit at the picking line and every five minutes take a scoop of peas, place them on a tray and register a variety of criteria as laid out on a given sheet. This was all part of quality control. No doubt the management had a use for it. Their names were Kieran who came from Dublin and Sean from Ballymena in Co. Antrim. Kieran was a tall gangly boy and a lot of fun and would greet us every morning with "How are yous all?" I was a bit wary of him at first suspecting he was more full of blarney than work but after a while he proved himself very reliable. Sean was a much quieter boy who kept himself to himself, just did his job, worked well, and presented his results as required according to the job specifications. Unlike Kieran who loved the adventure of visiting other places, Sean looked forward to going home. I admired them both, along with the other students for funding their education this way.

I had really looked forward to Sunday, for Tosh had said I could leave off early at 6 O'clock. From the glint in May's eye when he told me two days earlier I rather suspected she had something to do with it. I had arranged to take Josie to the Regent cinema in Norwich where Elvis Presley was starring in 'Love me Tender'. I coudn't be happier, but on arriving at work that morning I was met by a rather quiet and sombre lab. I was in a buoyant mood so I chirped "You can cheer up now. I'm here" but Steve's expression never changed as he said "There's been an accident" For a moment my mind raced. It couldn't be Josie. She wasn't coming in today. Had something happened to her last night and nobody's told me?

"It's Sean."

"Our Sean?"

"He was knocked down last night. He's dead."

"Dead! How? What? How did it happen?" Steve explained that being Saturday night last night a lot of the students had gone to the Scottow 'Three Horseshoes' pub for a 'jar' as they liked to call it, and it was whilst walking home along the dark country roads that Sean had been hit by one of the many lorries that went to and fro the factory. Death had been instantaneous. I was devastated and sat down to take it in. Yes I was relieved that nothing had happened to Josie but I couldn't take in the loss of such a young lad, just three years my junior, with so much life before him.

The rest of the day, inevitably was spent under a cloud and I was only too glad to get away at 6'O clock to pick up Josie, She was waiting for me as arranged and I broke the news to her. She didn't really know him but she could see that I was upset about it and she hugged me and said "You poor thing" and as I hugged her in return I thought of the transience of life and the tragedy of death and I knew that I loved her and wanted to be with her and protect her always.

We went to the cinema as planned, sitting as close together as the arm rests would allow, hand in hand, with a bag of sweets from the foyer: Josie's choice. We couldn't have been happier. The music and pathos evoked from Elvis Presley brought tears from Josie, but whether it was from the sheer pleasure of being with her combined with the sad news of the morning I must confess to a little dampness around the eyes myself. After the film we bought some chips and arm in arm we walked down to the river near Thorpe Station where we stood on the bridge and watched the reflection of the passing traffic in the water below.

"Mum says I must bring you in for a drink when we get back."

"She knows about me then?"

"Of course. I had to tell her where I was going tonight."

"And she didn't mind?"

"As long as I'm home by 11 O'clock."

"Then we'd better get going. I don't want to upset your mum." The journey back took a good half-hour and we only just made it. I wondered what kind of reception I'd get, especially when I saw a face at the curtain as we drew up. But I needn't have worried as her mum, herself a good looking woman of about 45, came to the door and ushered us in. Josie introduced me and I apologised for the lateness of the hour but she understood, said "As long as you're home safe" and added what I needed was a good hot drink before I set off again. Her father had already gone to bed as he worked on a farm and needed to get up early. Melanie too was nowhere to be seen and I presumed she too was in bed. We sat on a settee and drank our drinks whilst exchanging chit-chat. I could see the likeness of Josie in her, and hoped she wouldn't think of me as she did of Melanie's boyfriend Tom but I could tell she was weighing me up, a perfectly natural thing for a mother looking out for her girls. I didn't stay long and she motherly shooed me out, saying I had to get home and Josie needed her sleep, but I must come to tea sometime. On the doorstep I held Josie tight and kissed her and she said she had had a wonderful time, to which I wholeheartedly agreed, then she said goodnight and closed the door behind her. I went to my bike, put my gear on and switched on the lights. As I did so the downstairs lights in the cottage went out. I whispered "Goodnight Josie", got on my bike and drove away.

Chapter 7

Sean got his wish and was flown home to Ireland to his grieving parents and family. I felt so sorry for them. Yet another death in a country that was so used to it, but tragically this one occurred away from home where he should have been safe. I also felt sorry for the lorry driver who was involved in the accident. No blame was attributed to anyone. It was all just an unnecessary wasteful accident. Life continued as usual with plenty of willing students eager to do extra shifts and fill gaps.

My colour deficiency had never been a problem so far but it was about this time that I got caught out. Overblanching can be one cause of peas beginning to change colour from the fresh green we like to see on 'Garden Pea' adverts and on the labels of cans, to a browny tinge, whilst still containing their overall greenness. As I said before, those who have spent a lot of time, sometimes years, picking over peas on a belt, notice these subtle changes and I was called to the belt by the chargehand. She was a tall slim grey-haired lady called Betty who I always thought looked out of place here and would be better suited to posh tea parties or chairing W.I meetings but she was popular with the ladies and stood no nonsense. As I arrived she said "What's wrong with these peas then?"

I looked at them. "How do you mean?"

"They're brown."

"No they're not."

"Yes they are" I looked again. They looked just like any other peas I'd ever seen, and particularly millions I'd seen over the last 5 weeks. I wondered if I was having my leg pulled, it wouldn't be the first time.

"How do you mean brown?" I asked.

"Brown as in not green" she said, getting a little miffed. I looked at the ladies sitting at the belt for help but they all seemed to be on her side. Fortunately I was saved by the appearance of Tosh who always seemed to have an eye or ear for when something wasn't quite right. He looked at them, conceded that they were brownish, adjusted the blancher and all was well. Until this time I had never realised that, as I said earlier, although I can identify all primary and secondary colours, I still don't quite see colour as most other people do.

After this experience I was relieved when finally the last field was vined, the last hopper emptied, the last pea fell off the end of the last belt, and as the hymn says 'All is safely gathered in'. We were now in mid-July. *"What else had God to throw at us?"* His answer *"Stringless Beans"* It was as if one alien species had disappeared from our fields to be replaced with another. Not viners this time but strimmers, large round drums which like monsters consumed the stalks and leaves and spewed out the beans. Different shape, different taste but the same process, only difference being these were blanched by steam whereas the peas were blanched in hot water. These weren't the large, flat, beans familiar with gardeners and grown up beanstalks. No, these were rounded, firm and fleshy and easy to slice and the earth gave of its plenty.

Please don't think that I was beginning to regret coming to work here. Apart from the limited time with Josie, I loved every minute of it. Boredom never came into it. Everybody seemed to take the work in their stride and I rarely heard a raised voice in argument, and above all I was accepted as one of them.

My next task was to be accepted by Josie's family. The invitation to tea one day wasn't possible due to the hours I was working but a compromise had been reached, a supper after work on a Saturday evening. The feedback from Josie was that first impressions, that Sunday after the cinema, were good. But that of course was only from her mother. I was yet to meet her father.

"You don't have to come" Josie said "We can always make some excuse if you'd rather."

"No! Why should I? Let's do it. It'll be nice. I mean what

harm can they do me? No! don't answer that." We both laughed.

On the day, I bought some flowers from the shop just outside the factory gates, then at 8'O clock hurriedly put on a change of clothes I'd brought with me. I would have liked to shave but this was before the days of battery razors and there weren't the facilities or the time for a wet shave. Then I set off for their house. Arriving shortly after, Josie was there to meet me. She always managed to make my heart jump at the sight of her. Today she was in a body fitting pink dress and her hair with it's natural highlights danced in the sun as she moved her head from side to side. I hoped I'd managed to eliminate the smells of the factory with enough deodorant and aftershave to keep 'Boots' solvent and offset any lingering whiffs. She took my hand, and after gathering up my flowers and a brief kiss, she led me in.

Her parents were there, and Melanie, and the usual greetings were given as I presented the flowers to Mrs Fisher. She was delighted and thanked me profusely. I said I hoped they weren't too windswept as they had been in the pannier of my bike but she didn't seem to mind. Mr Fisher shook hands with me and I felt from his grip that he was a man used to manual labour. He was tall about 6 feet, wore glasses and was I thought rather shy in company. In fact I sensed this was a bigger ordeal for him than it was for me. Melanie said hello and I asked her how she was. She had a broader face than Josie and shorter hair but lovely features. I have always thought that pregnant women take on a bonny look but she looked a little drawn. Josie had told me that Melanie had suffered a lot from morning sickness and the smell of half cooked vegetables in the factory had been too much for her and she had had to give up work. I could sympathise with her about the smell.

"How's Tom?" I asked.

"He's fine" she said "He should be calling around later"

Some food had been laid out on a table in the garden and we went outside. Peter, Josie's dad, was very proud of his garden and offered to show me round. My dad was also a keen gardener so I had some interest and a little knowledge to help the conversation along. He was particularly proud of his vegetable garden and said he usually exhibited in the local village shows. I pleased him when I told him that his onions and carrots were far better than any my dad had ever managed to grow. I guessed it was because of the access to good farmyard manure but I didn't say so in case it detracted from his skill as a gardener. We sat or stood to eat rolls or sandwiches whilst Mrs. Fisher brought a pot of tea out. After giving me a cup and me saying "Thank you Mrs. Fisher" she said I could call her by her name Fiona as Mrs. Fisher made her sound too old. And catching Josie's eye and smiling, she said to her "And you can call me 'Mum'" which made everybody laugh and broke the ice.

They had gleaned quite a lot about me from Josie but, fair dues, I realised they wanted to hear more so I told them about my family: mother and father and two elder brothers, both married, one younger sister aged 16; father, a machinist in an engineering firm. We lived in an area of Norwich called the Heartsease, to the north east, so I was on the right side of the city to get to work.

All in all the evening passed quite pleasantly and it finished with Josie and I alone in the garden whilst her parents and Melanie went inside. We made the most of being together and Josie agreed the evening had gone well apart from the fact that there had been no sign of Tom, and Melanie was clearly upset and angry. They had a large garden and we walked away from the house to be alone before I left. As usual she smelt divine and felt so soft and fragile that I was afraid of crushing her in my arms. For once the fields were quiet, apart for the noise of night insects, and the air was warm and still as I held her.

"I love you Josie" I said and our eyes met, and as she said "And I love you too John, very much" we kissed our 'Goodnights'.

I said my goodbyes to everyone and thanked them for a lovely evening. Melanie had gone to bed having given up on Tom coming round. Josie saw me out and shortly I was on my

Frozen In Time

way. A few people were still about, heading home presumably. At the edge of the village a couple of lovers stood entwined by a wall and I smiled to myself and was as one with them in my love. As I passed the man looked up, and in my headlights, I couldn't be positive, but I swear that man was Tom.

Chapter 8

I didn't see Josie every day. Although my heart wanted to, my body needed a break from work. I just went home and collapsed. I didn't know whether to mention my suspicions about Tom to Josie. What if I was mistaken? I decided to keep quiet for the time being.

Cherries were one of the treats to come into the factory from the Westwick Estate. We didn't have a pipping machine so they weren't a very practicable proposition but we froze a few, and a few were put into large catering cans known as A10's. Other cans were A2½, A2's and A1's. The 'A' stands for American. There are 'E' cans for English but there is little call for them. The most common is the A2, suitable for most families.

A few cherries were pipped as samples by May and Phyllis in the lab and a lot were pipped by the rest of us as we tested them for flavour and put the pips in the bin.

Huge retorts were used to cook cans in and this was a very intricate and skilled job, which I learnt. Once the cans were all packed in on trays, huge doors were swung round and locked on with massive wing nuts. Then steam was injected and the cooking began. Governed by gauges the pressure had to be maintained. If they were allowed to go over pressure they could well blow off the door with the pressure of several tons; a potentially fatal scenario for anyone in front. More complicated was when the cooking was over. Cold water had to be let in. If it came in too soon it would condense the steam, create a vacuum, and the cans would burst. It could only be done by juggling the pressure gauges, quite an accomplishment which I learnt on the small one in the lab then progressed onto the big ones. This wasn't our job. We had retort men but it was very useful for them to have someone to call on in an emergency like an urgent toilet call.

Once the cans were out of the retorts they were sent over to the stores by our overhead railway system, but now the cans were no longer empty and therefore much heavier. I was standing there once going about my business when someone slapped me very hard on my back. I turned round to remonstrate. Jimmy was there laughing and I thought it was one of his jokes, then he pointed to a can rolling away on the floor. It had fallen off the rail above. "That was a near one" he chuckled. I was glad it had only been my back and not my head, and also glad that they didn't send the A10 cans overhead. This was when playing 'trains' became less fun.

I should perhaps at this time explain the relationship between Westwick Hall and the factory. Apparently the present Chairman of the Company, a Mr. Alexander was a Czech refugee during the war and coming to this country found work at the hall. Whether his name was Alexander or no I don't know. It doesn't sound very Czech. Anyway, so the story goes, he saw the potential for the food that the hall, and farm produced, being preserved through canning and later through freezing and he worked his way up to see it come to fruition. That is why fruit is still sent to the lab to be preserved for the hall and the estate provides vegetables to the factory.

Inside a secondary, smaller freezer, probably the original one before the factory expanded to it's present size there is a wire cage which contains all the special products the lab has produced. The cage is locked and only the lab staff had access. When we went down there we donned our duffel coat with hood and gloves and searched out what was required. Some things had been there for ages. There were some strange things in there, fish and meat as well as fruit. Amongst the fruit was the familiar named berry, to watchers of cartoons, of huckleberry. 'Huckleberry' like the word 'can' comes from America but they can be grown in this country, and indeed these were, in a field nearby. They look exactly like blackcurrants but instead of growing on bushes as blackcurrants are, they grow on plants not dissimilar to deadly nightshade and the berries from deadly nightshade are black also. Hence they never caught on for fear of confusing them. It was a risk no food producer here could take.

The beans continued to flow for 22 hours a day. Some were packed sliced, some whole. A different smell now pervaded the factory but it was never as obnoxious as the smell of sour peas had been. Because they were so small the peas could hide in every crevice in inaccessible places in machines and drains and just rot away. It was at least a week till we were really clear of them.

In mid August, soft fruit like black and red currants were brought in to be picked over and frozen. The canning line was a release valve. It was only brought into production in response to a lull in other production, or an order from a customer.

One such customer was Marks and Spencer. Every producer of food, sought a contract with them. Their quality was so high that being chosen to provide them was almost like receiving a Royal Appointment. Generally speaking we had nothing whatsoever to do with customers, that was the marketing side, but when Marks and Spencer is involved nothing is left to chance. They send their own team of inspectors down, lay down certain specifications, and they have to be obeyed. When we heard they were coming, the management could be seen everywhere. Suddenly men in red hats were on the factory floor, like bees round a honey pot, including the Managing Director.

I give no apology for the cleanliness and efficiency of the running of the canning line, it needed none, but for them it was not enough. They almost demanded clean overalls for every worker, every day, and everything that could be covered was, and if not it had a sheet of muslin put over it. This was actually a good idea over the syruper because it kept the wasps out, but for about a week our happy workforce was put under great strain by this relentless scrutiny. I don't know if we supplied them again after this, but if we didn't I don't think any of the factory workers would have minded.

Chapter 9

Towards the end of August I was making one of my regular calls to Josie. By now I was welcome and felt quite at home there. On arriving, it became apparent that something wasn't quite right. Josie was at the door with her mother who was clearly agitated.
"Whatever is the matter?" I asked alighting from my bike. Josie came to me, looking troubled.
"It's Melanie" she said.
"What about her?"
"We don't know where she is."
"How do you mean 'You don't know where she is'?" At this point Fiona, Josie's mum walked up to us.
"We may be worrying about nothing but she went out in rather a state."
"Where?"
"To see Tom. She had built herself up into such a state, said she was going to have it out with him."
"Have what out?" (as if I didn't know).
"She thinks he's been seeing someone else" Josie said. I tried to calm things down, "Well perhaps you're all worrying over nothing. How long has she been gone?"
"About an hour" said her mother.
" Well I expect she's talked to him, they've sorted it out, and now she's just stayed with him for a while" Even as I said it, I didn't believe a word of it, but I was trying to pour oil on troubled waters."Why don't Josie and I go and see where she is?"
"Would you?" she asked "It would put my mind at rest. I've not seen her like that before."
"Okay mum" said Josie "You go inside and we'll go to Tom's house and find her. She might come back here when we're gone. Don't worry. We'll find her and bring her home.

Everything will be alright." Her mother did as suggested and we set off walking to Tom's house. As we went I confided in Josie what I'd seen that night. She was horrified but added "I'm not surprised. That's the sort of thing he would do. He's got a bit of a reputation." Tom's house was not far. It was a rather unkempt farmhouse and we were met with two barking dogs. I was weary of them but Josie seemed to know them and calmed them down. However their barking brought Tom to the door without us knocking. He looked even surlier than I remembered him.

"Oh. It's you" he snapped.

"Have you seen Melanie?" asked Josie without waiting for niceties.

"Yes"

"Is she here?"

"No."

"Where is she then?"

"How the hell should I know?" he grunted. I interjected "How do you mean 'You don't know' If she came to see you, you must know where she is." He looked at me as if I didn't exist then turned to Josie.

"What she does is up to her. I told her I've finished with her. So there!" I could have punched him in the face. Unfortunately he would have probably wiped the floor with me.

"You bastard!" screamed Josie who was not so withholding and took a step forward only to have the door slammed in her face.

"Come away" I advised her "The important thing is to find Melanie. She obviously isn't here."

"But now I'm really worried" she said, almost in tears. "In her state she could do anything."

"Perhaps she's gone to friends. She must have friends in the village."

"Well yes Of course." We walked back down the driveway to the road. "She's got a friend called Gillian lives just down here. John be a dear and go to the end of the street upto the farm. I'll come and meet you eventually. That way we can cover more ground. Do you mind?"

"Not at all if it helps."

"Thanks love." She kissed me and we went our separate ways. I did as I was told, followed the street. There were a few houses with land in between but no sign of Melanie. It was as I came upto what looked like a neglected barn that I thought I heard something. I stopped and listened. Yes there it was again. I was sure it was the sound of someone sobbing. I walked down by the side of the barn towards the rear where the sound seemed to be coming from. "Melanie!" I said. "Melanie is that you?" There was a rustle as I turned the corner and there sitting on some straw on the ground was this sad, wretched girl crying her eyes out. "Oh Melanie this won't do will it?" I said as I went to her.

"Leave me alone."

"No I can't do that."

"Yes you can-leave me alone-I want to be alone." I stooped down beside her "Not like this you can't. Everyone's worried about you."

"Everyone? Does that include Tom?" She said that scornfully rather than hopefully. "Is he worried about me?"

"He would be if he saw you like this."

"He doesn't give a damn about me."

"Did he say that?"

"Yes he did. He's finished with me. He doesn't want me or my baby" At this she burst into tears again. "I may as well be dead." I sat down beside her on the straw and put my arm around her shoulder.

"That's a terrible thing to say."

"Why not? Why shouldn't I finish it all now?"

"Because too many people love you, that's why."

"But Tom doesn't."

"He's a fool. He's a stupid ignorant fool who doesn't know a beautiful girl when he sees one" She looked up at me.

"Do you think I'm beautiful?"

" I think you're extremely beautiful. Your hair's a mess" I

pushed it back off her face. "You've tears making streaks all down your face but underneath you're a beautiful person" I gave her my handkerchief. "Why don't you wipe your face?" She took it and dabbed at her eyes. But then she looked at me again and more tears appeared as she cried.

"But what am I going to do?" I took the handkerchief and wiped the new tears away.

"I think you've had a very lucky escape."

"How do you mean?"

"Well, you have had a very valuable lesson. You see, Inside you is another beautiful person."

"How do you know?"

"It stands to reason; beautiful mother, beautiful baby. Let me tell you something. My mother was in the same situation as you with my eldest brother."

"Was she?"

"Oh yes, but the father of the baby didn't want to know. He was a war baby and he left her soon after she was pregnant. She was devastated, just like you, but her family stood by her, and strangely enough a few months later she met my father, who took care of her and when the baby was born he brought him up as his own, and more than that, they had three other children, including me, and mum's never regretted not marrying the other fellow."

"But I love Tom."

"So you may, or you think you do, but my point Melanie is that if he doesn't want you in his life, he needn't be the end of yours. Somewhere out there is the most wonderful man you've yet to meet, and someday you will."

"Perhaps I have" she said looking up at me, And for a moment I thought she had the same look in her eyes that Josie had.

"You will Melanie-you will. Why don't we go home?" I helped her up and dusted her down and then she said "Are you going to marry Josie?" I was completely taken by surprise but smiling said "Probably."

"Good" she said "I'm glad. Otherwise I might have to marry

you myself" She smiled. I took her hand and we walked back to the road.

We met Josie along the road and she was so relieved and overjoyed she hugged her sister, asking if she was alright, telling her how worried she'd been, how worried mum had been, and it was a good job dad was out and she'd better get her home quickly before he came home. We soon returned home to the equally relieved mother who saw us coming. She hugged her and took her in, leaving Josie and I alone together for the first time that evening. There wasn't much of the evening left, so with our arms around each other we decided to just stroll for a while.

"Thank you John for finding Melanie" She said giving me a kiss as we walked.

"I'm only glad I did" I replied. We stopped at a field gate. Over the fields the sun was setting and the sky was a panorama of pink and orange and blue. "You were really worried about her, weren't you?" I said.

"Yes I was. She has always been one to make quick, sometimes rash decisions and after being treated the way she was by that moronic imbecile, who knows what she might have done." Her eyes flared with anger. "Do you know what I'd like to do to him. I'd like to...."

"Marry me" I said. She stopped in her tracks.

"What did you say?"

"I said I want you to marry me." All the fire had gone out of her. She went very quiet, pondering me with those eyes.

"Do you really mean it?" I pulled her to me.

"Of course I mean it. Josie I love you. I think you're the most wonderful girl in the world and I want you to be my wife." This time as she stared, a smile gradually crept over her face and suddenly she threw her arms around me and cried "Yes! yes! yes! Of course I'll marry you. I love you too John. Oh yes, yes I do." We hugged. We kissed. We held each other as the sun lost it's strength, disappeared over the horizon, and surrendered to the night. Now it was getting colder. Josie gave a shiver and happily we made our way back to the house.

"I want to tell the world" she said.

"And so you shall my darling, but tonight, I think, don't tell Melanie. I think she's been through enough." Josie saw the sense in this and I saw her to her door. As I did so her father appeared from along the road and walked up the path.

"Hello there" he grinned "Lovely evening" and he went indoors. We both laughed. He didn't know how wrong, and yet how right he was.

Chapter 10

The next 12 hours was like a dream, except I didn't sleep that much. I kept going over events of that night: what I had said, what Josie had said. Had she really said 'Yes' she'd marry me. I hadn't meant to blurt it out like that. I'd been thinking about asking her for some time but I had this preconception of proposals following special nights of wining and dining and we had little chance of that in our work, not at this time of year. Perhaps it was Melanie's plight and sorrow that made me want to feel secure with Josie, to know that she was mine for ever and always. Maybe that was a selfish reason, but my love for her was selfless. My aim was to make her happy, and that I fully intended to do.

Work began on the day shift at 8a.m. I had several machines to get started so I attended to them. As soon as I was free I set out to find Josie. I found her eventually at the far end of the factory with her usual crowd stapling up boxes. A huge foot stapler was used for this. It rose about four feet in the air and you placed the boxes on an outstretched arm and pressed down with your foot. It was a standing up job and it worked with great effect to change boxes from flat-pack to useable containers. I sidled up to her.

"You alright?" I asked.

"No" she answered, not smiling.

"Why?" I said, feeling panic set in. "What's happened?"

"I got engaged last night" and a broad grin spread over her face "At least, I think I did."

"Oh you certainly did. You can bet on it. You had me worried then. Don't ever do that to me again" She smiled "Sorry" and I asked "Does anybody else know?"

"Only mum. I told her this morning."

"And?"

"She was pleased."

"Well that's good anyway. You know I meant what I said last night."

"I hope so."

"No. I mean you can tell who you like. I don't mind. I want everyone to know how lucky I am." And then as so often happened Christine appeared.

"Oh not you again. You know, I don't know why you two don't get married, you're as good as, you're always together. Haven't you got a blancher to check or something?" I grinned and went on my way to the laughter of all the other girls.

Twenty minutes later Christine came bursting in to the lab. Confronting Tosh, she pointed to me. "Have you heard what he's done?"

Tosh looked concerned. May and Phyllis stopped working and looked surprised. I looked worried. "*What have I done?*" Surely I hadn't made an error on the blancher settings. Had I started up the wrong one? What was it?

"What's he done?" enquired Tosh always ready to give his staff all his support.

"Only gone and pinched one of my girls" she continued. Everybody looked baffled and looked at me. "As in, got engaged to Josie last night" and with a broad grin she came over to me, gave me a hug and a kiss and said "It's great news I couldn't be happier for you both. You see, people do take my advice sometimes." Tosh, May and Phyllis joined in the congratulations and I felt myself reddening with embarrassment. So Josie had shared her good news. I could look forward to a day of leg-pulling that was for sure but I felt an inner warmth of happiness at the prospect.

"It was the beginning of September and the pressure in the factory was easing off, noticeable by the fewer number of students that could be seen. Many had left with either pockets full of money, or, if they were wise, receipts for money already banked. The night shift continued for a while longer as calabrese, cauliflower and carrots added to the last fields of beans. On the fruit side, blackberries were arriving, huge, black, cultivated ones, a sure sign of Autumn fast approaching. Plums also, yellow and purple Pershores, ideal for canning, arrived in their thousands. Fruit of course does not need blanching so it needs less work than vegetables. And in the lab each new product added to our store of finest samples the company could produce and kept May and Phyllis in work and gave myself further opportunity to do some canning.

Getting engaged is a matter between two people, an agreement to get married sometime. Getting married is something else. In the sixties, those under 21 years old needed parents' permission. Josie was 18, coming up to 19 this September. I hadn't asked her parents if we could get engaged, I didn't need to. Getting married in the next two years I would have to. I hoped there would be no problem because neither of us wanted to wait that long. Our love was a passionate one and waiting would be difficult.

So far my parents, and family hadn't met Josie. It had simply not been possible for me to introduce her to them. I had told them about her naturally enough and now I had broken the news that we were engaged. They, equally naturally, wanted to meet her and I had promised them they would as soon as work permitted. Also, like all newly engaged women, Josie wanted a ring to show off and I desperately wanted to give her one but I wanted us to choose it together. So we had planned that the first Sunday we were both free we would go to meet my parents and the first Saturday free we would choose the ring.

Sunday came first. Two weeks into September we got the day off. I had agreed with Josie that she should catch the train from Worstead Station in the afternoon and I would meet her at Norwich Thorpe Station. I waited for her at the appointed time and was truly stunned by her appearance as she walked off the platform to meet me. She wore a maroon flared skirt with jacket to match over a white blouse with frills down the front. We kissed and hand in hand made our way to where the bike was parked. I kept a spare jacket for her in the pannier and a helmet of course and soon we were on our way. There are many ways of getting to our destination and I chose the scenic route. This way led us through the famous Mousehold Heath where we took a detour to stop in front of Norwich Prison from where we had spectacular views of the city with its Cathedral and Castle Museum. We then continued to my home.

"Are you nervous?" I asked as I retrieved the coat and helmet and let her straighten herself from the journey.

"A bit" she said but I assured her that she had nothing to fear and we went in. I hadn't expected them all to be there but they were: mum, dad, elder brothers Philip and Keith and sister Karen. They had all come to see who I was about to bring into the family. Philip the oldest was married. He was a postman and although he didn't know Sloley personally he knew of all the villages round there from sorting mail. Keith was a builder, also married, and Karen who was just sixteen hadn't yet decided what she wanted to do and was working in a shop meanwhile. The greetings were cordial and friendly and Josie who was overwhelmed at first soon settled down and by tea time was on good terms with all. My eldest brother caught me alone in the kitchen at one time and said "Very nice. Very nice indeed" And I heard later that that was the verdict of them all. Karen, who was of course the only girl in the family, relished the idea of another female with whom to communicate. We didn't stay too long after tea. For one thing I thought it was long enough for the first time and for another I wanted her to myself for a while, plus I was taking her home and didn't want to be late. We said our goodbyes, with not a few kisses, especially from my brothers, and with mum saying "Hope to see you soon" we set off for the country.

I took the Wroxham Rd. for a change. It was a warm evening and we stopped at Wroxham to look at the river. Wroxham is probably the heart of the broads and certainly the main shopping centre. It was full of Broads cruisers and holiday makers here for cruising holidays. Then turning left through Wroxham we headed for Coltishall. Just before we got there the river comes very close to the road by a pub which caters for the passing river and road trade. Once again we stopped and sat on our coats by the river bank watching small craft and larger cruisers passing by. Josie laid back with her head on my lap and after a short while she said ""Does Philip know who his real father is?"

"Pardon?" I said.

"Melanie told me what you said about how your dad adopted him as his own." I began to laugh. "What are you laughing at?" she queried, mystified.

"He wasn't adopted." I said "I made it all up." She sat up.

"You made it up. Why?"

"I had to say something. She was in such a state. I was trying to show her that things aren't always as bad as you think they are." She looked at me.

"Now I know why I love you John Clark" and she gave me the most delicious kiss to which I responded willingly. We only parted when we heard a boat horn sounding and looking up saw several people whooping and waving their approval. We waved back and cuddled closer till the evening midges took a fancy to us and we decided it was time to head for home.

Chapter 11

I had been thinking for some time that I needed to update my mode of transport. My N.S.U. Quickly had served us well but it was after all just a moped, albeit a strong one doing the work of a motor-bike. When I saw a good trade in deal for a Scooter, a Lambretta, I decided to go for it. I was never a speed merchant but I thought Josie would prefer it to the moped and of course with it's rising front and large windscreen it would be a much drier affair and hopefully warmer in the coming Winter. I took it to work naturally, and Josie was indeed impressed. I had also planned a day out on the Saturday of our official engagement and felt sure this would suit us better. There were a few jibes as to whether I was a 'Mod' or a 'Rocker' for this was the era of the scooter fraternity that terrorised some of our seaside resorts. But I assured everyone that mine was for purely peaceful means, and pleasure of course.

There were some interesting characters, other than those I've already mentioned, in various other parts of the factory. The Electrical Dept. was part of the Workshop and one electrician I remember, name of Sydney, was one of them. His expression was always deadpan and if he did smile it was when he thought he'd told you something you didn't know. He was a bit like a camel. Let me explain-Arabs claim to know 99 names of god but as one satirist said, the camel smiles because he knows the hundredth. Well he was like that. He very rarely laughed but he gave the impression of being a contented man. I enjoyed philosophical discussions with him. On the subject of religion and infinity he argued that infinity was just two inches long. His argument went like this. If you cut a piece of paper two inches long into halves, then cut one half into halves again and continued halving, you could in theory keep cutting each space in half forever, albeit they would be micro and mini-micro cuts and you would never move out of the two inches. The cuts would be infinitesimal i.e. infinity is two inches. The same argument would be true of any length but it was an interesting thought. Then we were discussing the wonders of the human brain. And I said that I'd heard that to make a machine capable of doing what the human brain could, would require the power of Niagara Falls to run it and the waters of Niagara to cool it. He replied that that was without the use of trasformers. Well he was the electrician. I bowed to his knowledge.

As regards having a Saturday off, Tosh and I came to an agreement. He was very much a family man and a gardener and had missed both during the summer. By now I was considered capable of covering a shift alone so he suggested that he would cover me for the Saturday If I covered him for the Sunday, a plan I readily acceded to. As it happened it coincided with Josie's birthday so it suited us perfectly. I broke the news to Josie when I saw her and she was delighted. "I can't wait" she said "but I do hope the weather changes" for it was now Thursday and it was pouring down outside. Fortunately though the forecast was promising.

I haven't mentioned Steve much because he was still doing the nightshift and I didn't see much of him. He reported to us what had gone on during the night before he signed off each morning and we did the same in the evening, thus we kept up to date with all major and minor events. I didn't envy him the night shift at all but I had been warned that next year I would have to do my share. I didn't much fancy it though for I had once done a night shift of just one night and I didn't enjoy it at all. Mind you the circumstances were very different. It was in the Tax Office, strangely enough. A memo came round saying the office needed redecorating and it suited the Revenue to have it done at night in case the decorators overheard something they shouldn't. Equally they needed tax officers to be there with them during the night so that they didn't snoop into confidential files. Volunteers were requested. We didn't have to do anything, just be there and we would be recompensed for the inconvenient hours. I volunteered. Why not? It was an horrendous night, utter boredom and keeping awake was nearly impossible. The painters laughed and said I had eyes like gob-stoppers. It was the longest night I remember and I vowed never to volunteer again. Still Steve seemed to like it. He always said that management sleeps when you're doing nights. You get little or no hassle from them.

Saturday morning shone sunny and warm. I had polished the scooter so it shone and we'd agreed to meet at Josie's early to make the most of the day. I was there at 9.30. Her mother let me in and she told me Josie wasn't quite ready. I was giving her some idea of what we planned to do that day when Josie appeared downstairs. She was wearing a yellow cotton dress that her parents had bought her for her birthday. It had a square neck with a flared skirt which stood out due to a stiff petticoat beneath, which I didn't know at the time. She looked wonderful and I told her so, wished her happy birthday and gave her a card and a kiss. Melanie came downstairs then and added her approval, as did her mother, and I sensed the pride she had in her as she saw her standing there. She put on a cardigan and we went out. It seemed a shame to cover her with a bike jacket but it was only for the ride, and we set off for North Walsham.

Since our engagement we had talked a lot about money and the need to save so we had agreed not to overspend on a ring. We parked the bike and headed for the High St. by way of the churchyard. Josie was having trouble with her underskirt which kept dropping a few inches so we stopped somewhere discreetly so she could readjust it then we made our way to the jewellers. We looked in at the jeweller's window to see the range of rings then we went inside to let the salesman do his best with our limited resources. I wanted to give her the world but unfortunately it wasn't in my pocket. This was a new experience for me, and within our budget, Josie was delighted with a diamond ring. She wanted me to have one too so I purchased a gold ring to keep her happy. I remember mine cost

£5, hers was more expensive. She insisted on paying for it, saying it had no meaning otherwise.

We left the shop wearing our rings and made for a cake shop to buy some rolls and a cake for lunch to take with us. Josie was still having trouble with her underskirt having dropped another two inches so we stepped into a passageway to enable her to pull it up. In the cake shop we made our purchases and Josie had reached her patience with the underskirt so she decided enough was enough and when she thought no one was looking she quickly removed it, rolled it up, smiled at the shop assistant and off we went.

It was getting warmer so she didn't miss the extra layer as we set off for Mundesley the nearest seaside place to here. It was to be a day to remember, no underskirts, no overheads, just God's good sea, sand and sky and two people deeply in love.

We walked down the cliff path to the beach and made our claim to a part of beach where we had relatively few neighbours and spreading ourselves out took off our shoes and lay down in the sun and relaxed, Josie admiring the reflection of the sun's rays in the ring on her finger. After a while we strolled down to the sea and hand in hand walked along the tidal edge before returning once more to our belongings and lying down.

I remember Mundesley from Sunday School outings many years ago. It was popular for such events, with games on the beach and strawberry teas in the church hall. It hadn't changed much.

After that we set off again along the coast to a place called Happisburgh (pronounced Haysborough). This was another place I was familiar with having camped in a field near here when I was 14. Happisburgh is dominated by it's red and white barber pole, striped lighthouse, set there because of dangerous sand banks off the coast. It wasn't as popular as other resorts, not having the facilities, but then we weren't looking for company. Taking our food with us we bought a cold drink from the shop and settled down on the beach to eat our lunch. Josie was more familiar with this coast than me, living so much nearer, and she told me how off this coast H.M.S. Invincible on its way to join Nelson had struck a sandbank and gone down with over a hundred lives. She had learnt it on a school trip and the horror of it had stayed with her. I just thought '*so much for being invincible*' and '*what the hell was the lighthouse keeper doing at the time?*'. Looking at the sea as it gently rolled in, for us it was nothing but amicable, and gentle, and peaceful.

We stayed there for an hour or two before proceeding along the coast road to another Sunday School Outing haunt, Sea Palling. Here again things hadn't changed since I had come here many years before. The entrance to the beach was over a concrete bridge set between natural sea defences of sand banks and marram grass. As before we made a base along the beach and then we walked, we ran, we teased each other at the water's edge then we collapsed amidst our few belongings and lay in each other's arms and for a while we even slept. Before we left we had a last stroll along the beach and for us we knew tomorrow was back at work but today there was no work, no worry, no Westwick.

Our return journey took us through Stalham, an old market town set on the River Ant. Here we stopped and had tea and a cake in a café overlooking the water. We had completed a circular route with only a few more miles to go to home. Josie still kept admiring her ring and was now keen to show it off to her family. We finished our tea and headed for home, through Smallburgh and across country to reach her house around five o'clock.

There was much excitement amongst the women as they admired the ring, even though I'm sure it wasn't the biggest they'd ever seen, and when Josie told them about the saga of the underskirt they all had a big laugh and her mum said she'd fix it. For a birthday surprise a tea had been prepared, even though they had no idea when we'd return, and after Josie had gone upstairs to wash and change from the heat and sweat of the day we all enjoyed the special treat, including birthday

Frozen In Time

cake which her mother had made. For me it had been a most memorable day and one I shall never forget.

Chapter 12

Wearing rings at work was not a good idea, especially in the food industry where the product can dislodge or destroy the delicate settings but one can forgive Josie for wanting to show hers off, which of course she did at the first opportunity. After the obligatory 'Oohs!' and 'Aahs!' the question was put "When are you going to get married?" To which the answer was "We don't know." We didn't know because: one, we needed somewhere to live ; and two, we hadn't broached the subject to her parents. They may have been happy for us to name a date but the thought that they might not, rather made me wary of mentioning it. Still the engagement was the first step. At least everyone knew our intentions.

The danger of wearing rings doesn't only apply to the female sex, as I discovered to my cost. We were now entering the sprout season, of which the factory had a large intake. These were blanched by steam on the metal conveyor in the same way as mushrooms. And in the same way they were tested in the lab for enzyme activity. Like the mushrooms they were cut in half and placed in a petri dish to assess the degree of blanch. If no colour showed we had blanched too much, they were cooked. If the whole inside coloured, they were still raw and if just a little showed, we were about right.

The easiest way to see what was going on was to manfully climb up on the blancher. There were no steps. We stood on pipes and pulled ourselves up to view the various food on the belt. It was on such an occasion that holding on the top of the blancher I attempted to come down. I'd done it dozens of times. I knew where to put my feet and how to jump down. So I did. The trouble was, I came down but my hand didn't. Unused to wearing a ring it had caught on the lip of the blancher's side and wanted to stay. The pain was excruciating and I struggled to get my footing back on the blancher's side which I did and lifting my finger released it from it's grip. I thought it was broken and in agony went to the first aid room where the nurse checked it and treated it and proclaimed it sore but sound. I was very lucky and realised my ring and I had better coordinate our actions in future.

Sprouts were the big veg. intake of the Autumn. They were riddled to give large, medium or small and they occupied the main inspection lines through October and into November. Apples were the new fruit that had to be dealt with. Bramleys were the preferred variety and a clever machine had been designed to deal with them. They were different from every other fruit we processed in that they had to be peeled and cored. I don't know if you've ever peeled an apple and tried to do what we did as children. When helping our mother do this task we made a game of it. The object was to peel the whole apple and only end up with one piece of connected peel. Modern peelers can do it better but with a knife it was quite a challenge. I've even known it be used as a party game.

In effect, this is what the machine peeler did. The apple was rammed onto a spike which rotated the apple. A blade, which was sprung to move with the size of the apple, shaved off the peel whilst moving down it, then it was down to the ladies on the belt to remove any bits or blemishes that had escaped the knife.

The other problem with apples as every housewife knows is that as soon as apples are peeled they begin to yellow. That is they oxidise. To prevent this they are placed in a 2% brine solution which preserves their whiteness, Strangely enough the salt is so weak that it never taints the fruit.

I never knew what happened to all those apple peels. No doubt someone paid, or was paid, to take it away for compost or to feed the pigs. No doubt that's why apple sauce goes so well with roast pork.

The nightshift came to an end, the students had all packed up and gone and our hours became more civilised. It was good to have Steve back. He brought a sense of fun to the job which Tosh, being the boss, couldn't. We were more of a team when he was there. We did things together instead of in isolation. He was also known to play jokes when the opportunity arose. One of the jobs we had to do was send frozen samples to various places. To do this we had to place them in a box and surround them with a substance called cardice. This is simply solidified carbon dioxide and is as cold as ice. As the cardice melts it gives off the gas carbon dioxide which, because it is cold, it looks and feels like mist or fog. This is the same thing used on stage to create misty scenes. Now if you placed a piece of this in a sealed container like a can, the gas would build up such a pressure that eventually the lid would pop off with an almighty bang. This could be dangerous but if you placed it inside a cardboard box you would get the explosion without any danger, other than a heart attack that is. Christine was also glad to see Steve back and was not adverse to the odd prank too and it was on her that he played this one. Obviously the warmer the ice gets the quicker the can will blow and it's not easy to calculate the time it takes to do this. Having prepared it he put it under a bench near the lab and called her over. Then he engaged her in conversation on some pretence or other and hoped it would blow. It did. Christine jumped forward from the shock. "Oh my god! What was that?" she said turning around, only to see white fumes escaping from a cardboard box and to hear the uncontrolled laughter coming from Steve.

"You bastard!" she said, her hand across her chest, but she was smiling now. "I'll get you for this just you wait and see," and she walked away planning her revenge.

'Springers' is the name given to cans that explode of their own accord. This happens for various reasons: insufficient exhausting, wrong cooking time, leaky can, poor seal, anything that allows bacteria to breed. When this happens the lid of the can will feel sprung. If you ever see one in a shop which has that bowed feel to it don't buy it. Generally speaking the first sign of it happening in the store is when a box is seen to be leaking and the offending can or cans removed. Every so often we were sent all the sprung cans that had been discovered for us to destroy. This was quite fun, for the workshop had made a device from a steel file with a point and put a shield on it as big as a plate so it looked a bit like a dagger. We then took the sprung cans to a piece of dirt ground away from the factory and proceeded to stab them. The fun was, that depending on how far gone they were, you could usually expect a fountain of different coloured juices shooting up into the air. The plate shield protected you from the initial blast and gave you time to move away before the display. Peas from A10 cans, the catering ones, were the best because they shot up the highest, then a pea would get stuck in the hole, pressure would build up behind it and away it would go again. The downside was the appalling smell from putrid peas. Fortunately we didn't get many bad cans, but it was a little light relief when we did.

Chapter 13

The shortened working hours gave Josie and I more time together after work. I frequently stayed for tea, or dinner, depending on what was provided, so that I didn't need to go all the way to Norwich and come back in the evening. This worked well if we wanted to go out for the evening, to the cinema for example. Melanie was now 6 months pregnant and showing it. There had been no reconciliation with Tom, which pleased us all, and she had now accepted it. Much of the time we spent at home, with the colder evenings upon us, but there was little privacy. In fact the only private moments were after everybody else had gone to bed, or if her parents and Melanie were out, which wasn't often. Josie was adamant that sex was to be after marriage and I respected her for that. She didn't want to end up like Melanie. But if sex was to be later, I wanted marriage to be sooner. So we discussed it and I agreed that the right thing was to ask her father if we could get married as soon as reasonably possible. It was a Saturday morning when the opportunity presented itself. Her father was in the garden so with a prompt from Josie I bit the bullet and went out to talk to him. This was a first for both of us. As with most things in life there are no rehearsals. I didn't go straight into it but prevaricated talking about the garden, assessing his mood, then I asked him. "Josie and I would like to get married as soon as possible but we need your permission as she's only 19."

"Nothing to do with me lad" he remarked "better ask her mother, that's her department. Makes no difference to me" and he carried on gardening. I didn't know what to say to that so I just said.

"Oh. Right. I'll do that" and went back indoors. Josie met me.

"What did he say?"

"Well I think it was a yes but he's put the onus on your mum. Says its up to her."

"Typical. Likes the easy life does my dad. Well off you go then."

"What now?"

"Yes. She's in the kitchen. Ask her now. Strike whilst the iron is hot." I didn't like the sound of that word 'strike' but I went anyway. Somehow I relished this less than asking her dad. Man to man seemed alright but man to woman was a little daunting. I entered the kitchen. Her mother was busy at the sink and she smiled at me. I went straight for it.

"There's something I want to ask you."

"Yes dear, what is it?"

"Will you expect us to wait till Josie is 21 before we get married? Only we'd rather not wait that long." She wiped her hands on a tea towel, suggesting to me that important decisions can't be made with wet hands, then she said, "Provided you can find somewhere to live I have no objections."

"Really?" I said, not believing my ears.

"But you won't find accomodation round here very easy to come by. It's in short supply and you won't want to travel to work I hope."

"No I don't. I want to live around here. I like it here."

"And weddings cost a lot of money so unless you have some savings you'd better be prepared to wait."

I went back to Josie.

"Well?" she asked anxiously.

"Well" I replied "At least she hasn't said no, but she doesn't think it likely just yet."

"Why not?"

"Two reasons, money and housing, and we haven't got either."

"I've got some."

"So have I, but not enough for a wedding."

"But if we carry on saving we can do it."

"We'll have to make do with nights in."

"That doesn't bother me."

"And somewhere to live, that could be a problem."
"But we'll find something John. I promise you we will" and she held me close.
"Of course we will Josie." but as I hugged her in return, inwardly I wasn't so sure.

The private freezer cage in which special packs were kept, also served another purpose. It came in handy for Tosh's personal use. As I said he was a very keen gardener and his interest included keeping chickens. They kept his family supplied with eggs, but they weren't pets. When their egg laying days were over he would have them all killed, plucked, dressed, and they would end up deep frozen for his family needs. Then he would replace them with new stock, or should I say flock.

But Tosh was not one to pass up on other food opportunities. I remember one day he arrived at the lab with something wrapped in newspaper. When he unwrapped it on the workbench in front of the ladies we were all surprised to see a prize pike staring up at us. Apparently a friend had caught it over the weekend and after the initial euphoria of the catch he wanted to get rid of it and Tosh was the obvious choice. So here it was a job for the ladies, to clean it, fillet it, chop it up into edible chunks and pop it in the freezer.

After looking at it warily for a moment, Phyllis, who was game for anything, picked up a knife and began to remove some of the scales by running the knife up it's back. All of a sudden there was an enormous scream. Phyllis jumped back and we all looked. The pike was alive. It reared up it's head, opened it's mouth, raised its tail in the air then thumped it down on the bench. Phyllis was a nervous wreck.

"The bloody thing's still alive!" she screamed. We all looked in amazement.

"But it can't be" said Tosh, "It's been out of the water since Saturday and this is Monday."

"Well you saw it" she answered, "I'm not going anywhere near it" and she wouldn't. So Tosh took the knife from her and swiftly cut off it's head.

Frozen In Time

"Well it's dead now" he said. We concluded that it had been dead but what had happened was by scraping up the fish's backbone Phyllis had stimulated the spinal chord which had brought about the amazing reaction. It did eventually end up in the freezer.

Chapter 14

The period leading up to Christmas was a quiet one. Only the regular ladies remained after the night shift and seasonal workers had left, and they were kept occupied by packing food that had been frozen in haste during the rush of the summer. The canning line too was kept busy with both fruit and veg. Life was altogether at a more leisurely pace. Josie and I kept to our intentions of minimum expenditure and maximum saving. The earliest date for a wedding would be Spring next year but that still depended on the criteria already mentioned, housing and money. We knew that if we didn't wed then there would be no chance during the busy season which would take us to next Autumn, a year away. We neither of us wanted to wait that long.

The week before Christmas saw the usual lightening of attitude to work as people began to get into the festive spirit. We were able to spend a whole hour in the canteen for our lunch without getting called out once. Usually the men sat together on their tables whilst the women did the same. One rowdy bunch of girls, led by a married girl in her twenties called Brenda were making innuendoes to our table, made up of engineers, freezer men and factory floor staff, when Brenda took it on herself to come to our table and proceed to kiss everyone on it. The kisses weren't just pecks either, they were full mouth smackers. I knew Josie was somewhere in the canteen and probably watching all of this. Most of the men were married men and just enjoyed it but when she came to me I declined. This did not please her and she returned to her table a little put out. One of my companions said to me "Now you've done it John. You've made her even more determined to come on to you, a woman scorned and all that. You'd better watch out" and they all laughed. Little did I know how right they were.

Frozen In Time

It was Christmas Eve and work was grinding to a halt with the anticipation of the Christmas break. I was staying with Josie till Boxing Day, when she was coming to my parent's house. I would be sleeping on the settee but I didn't mind. Just to be with her would be bliss. I was on a last minute trip to the freezer store to get things required for people for the Christmas fare. A few girls were wandering the factory on the prowl. The charge hands had virtually given up any hope of getting work done. I entered the freezer and closed the door behind me. I was opening our cage when I heard someone open the freezer door. Turning round I was surprised to see Brenda standing there. "What do you want?" I asked. She closed the door. "It's cold in here isn't it." she said.

"Yes." I replied "and you shouldn't be in here."

"But it's more private in here, and you do want us to be private don't you ?" she sidled up to me and I could tell she'd had a drink or two.

"You'll catch your death in here" I said.

"Not if you keep me warm" she whispered and I knew I was in trouble. I had to get her out of here before someone saw us, before someone told Josie. How would I explain this? Would she ever believe me? Quickly I turned her round and ushered her to the door.

"Oh don't be a spoilsport" she exclaimed "It is Christmas after all." I managed to open the door despite her protestations and noticing there was nobody about I edged her out. "Happy Christmas" I said and closed the door. I didn't see her again, even after Christmas. Somebody said that she'd been having a tough time with her husband and they had decided to move away and start again. I hope they managed it.

I returned to the lab with the required items and suffered no other mishaps. Tosh had his own Christmas ritual. Our store of cans, which were special samples, were all code dated. So Tosh looked through them and took out those that had the earliest code and put them into boxes that held twelve cans each. This was his present to each of us, and a very welcome gift it was too. Usually they would be fruit rather than veg. but all were welcome.

But there was a rather bizarre ceremony still to come. I had never seen our Chairman Mr. Alexander but that was about to change. The shift ended and everyone made their way happily to their homes. We wished May and Phyllis 'Happy Christmas' and they went home to their families, but we had to stay. Tosh had told me that the Chairman came to the factory to present gifts to all the staff i.e. the green hats, as appreciation for our hard work during the year.

We all gathered in the one office that could hold us all and waited. Mr. Alexander arrived. He was a man in his sixties, balding with glasses, but a cheerful face, accompanied by the Managing Director and Rupert Beard the Works Manager. He said a few words of gratitude and best wishes then began the gift ceremony. In keeping with the company's business, that of freezing, all the gifts were frozen, frozen fowl. Depending on your seniority of service so was your bird's size dictated. Be it chicken, goose or turkey the more years you'd been there the bigger the bird you got. But what was bizarre about it was the way you were presented with them. He literally threw it at you. I was alright. I hadn't been there a year and had no trouble catching a chicken but people like Tosh had a harder job catching a large turkey. The advantage was, the bigger the bird, the harder he found it to throw, so it balanced out really. One or two found their way onto the floor. Neither was he any gentler on the ladies. They had to struggle like the rest. The ritual over we wished each other a Happy Christmas and went on our way.

I made my way to Josie's. She'd gone home at the end of the shift. I didn't like her travelling home in the dark along those country roads but she reminded me she was a country girl and used to it. I didn't take the chicken. It was too late to thaw it out for Christmas Day so I put it in the lab freezer for later but I took the cans. They would come in handy, plus presents I'd got for the family. Josie's parents weren't wealthy but they were generous, and they made this a Christmas to remember.

Frozen In Time

In the evening we played Monopoly and I soon learned that dealing in property was something I knew nothing about and I was the first to be bankrupt. Melanie was a little bit weepy due to her condition and the circumstances of them but we did our best to cheer her up and by the end of the evening she was crying with laughter as much as with melancholia. We laughed well into the night before everybody turned in. Fiona brought a pillow, sheets and blankets for me on the settee and Josie and I had a few minutes together before we wished each other a 'Happy Christmas darling' and she went to bed. I made a sort of bed and laid down thinking how happy and lucky I was, and how close Josie was, and longing for her to be beside me, I fell asleep.

Christmas morning started early with Fiona busy in the kitchen getting the turkey in the oven to ensure the full cooking time. I could easily have turned over and gone to sleep but having tried that once in the night and ending up on the floor I decided I ought to get up and release the living room to through traffic. The girls had no such need and arrived downstairs a good hour later. Even early in the morning Josie looked lovely and we kissed and exchanged gifts. I had bought Josie a blue and white quilted dressing gown and she bought me a pair of leather gloves to wear on the scooter. Other gifts were exchanged and then Fiona gave us an envelope between us. Josie opened it. In it was £20 from her and Peter. "We thought it might encourage your saving" she said. We of course were delighted and we thanked them both profusely. Twenty pounds at that time was nearly two weeks wages for a farm worker. They had been very generous indeed.

    We had a small breakfast then Josie and I went for a walk in the crisp December air, whilst Melanie helped her mother with the meal preparations. We did offer to help, but with the words "Too many cooks......" from Fiona we excused ourselves. We strolled along arm in arm. As we passed a farm we saw cows being released from milking sheds where they had given of their milk and were reminded that even on Christmas

Day some people still had to work. Others were out too, building up an appetite for lunch. We were on nodding acquaintance with a few of them. Some were strangers, probably visiting relatives for the holiday. "That was a lovely gift your parents gave us" I said.

"I had no idea they were going to do that. At least it shows us that they are behind us in our plans."

"More than that. I think we should seriously look at what's available to rent. At least we should get some idea of what we're up against" Happy with that idea we made our way back with renewed appetite for lunch and lodgings.

Christmas lunch was everything one expects it to be, turkey with all the trimmings, followed by Christmas pud. and cream, and afterwards Josie and I did the washing up whilst her parents and Melanie relaxed in front of a roaring wood fire. Then we joined them and we all sat watching the television in between dozing. The rest of the day passed all too quickly. In the evening we played cards and I showed much more prowess at this than the night before. Finally we watched something else on the telly before I began my second night on the settee. At least I had the advantage of a warm room, whilst in a house with no central heating, the bedrooms were a bit chilly. Gladly would I have shared my warmth with Josie, but that was only one of the dreams I had that night.

Boxing Day we set out for Norwich to see my parents. I thanked Fiona and Peter for the lovely time I had had and they said that before long they would like to meet my parents which I promised them I would try and arrange. Dressed up against the cold we set off and in half an hour we were safely there. My parents and Karen were there and they made us welcome with a warm drink. There was more present giving and Karen enjoyed showing Josie what she had received, especially girlie things. Josie was staying the night and was to share a bed with Karen, or sleep on the floor, the choice was hers. The house was decorated to the limit and sweets, fruit and other goodies were evident everywhere. My parents had always had this idea about Christmas which I found a little ironic. For about a month before Christmas Mum would buy food of all kinds for the occasion and on no account were we to touch any of it. Then starting on Christmas Eve it all suddenly appeared and woe betide you if you didn't touch it. I suppose it all stems from the war when treats were hard to come by and you had to buy when available and stockpile for Christmas. We had a meal of cold meat and pickles, traditional for Boxing Day and in the afternoon my eldest brother Philip came round with his wife Helen and Josie was introduced to her. We all got on together. Karen particularly enjoying Josie's company and putting in her request to be a bridesmaid at our wedding. She kindly said that no plans were made yet but she was sure she could be. Everybody took to Josie which made me very pleased and when my dad saw me, out of Josie's hearing, he said he thought I'd made a good choice. I broached the matter of the two sets of parents meeting sometime and they were willing to go along with it, though they didn't think there was any hurry. It wasn't something I was going to push for. The evening came and went with the usual tea that nobody wanted much of, crackers and funny hats which I soon discarded. Having to wear one at work was bad enough. Then eventually we went to our separate rooms. Mine was next to Karen's and Josie gave me a view of herself in the dressing gown I had bought her. The blue in it brought out the blue in her eyes and made her even more alluring. We kissed good night and went to bed and for sometime I could hear the two girls chattering away and laughing till finally all was quiet.

We left after breakfast the next day to go back to Sloley. I was glad to be going. I had shown Josie to my family but now I wanted her to myself. I wanted everyone to love her as I did but I didn't want to share her, like a favourite toy you want everyone else to admire without relinquishing it. Romantic love is selfish, I know that. Real love is not selfish. It will give and give and give, even without return, and therein is the dilemma. I suppose that where the two meet and coexist is what we call true love. Time and years will no doubt tip the balance towards the latter but for now I wanted to enjoy the former.

Chapter 15

For some people, returning to work after Christmas is just what they need. Two or three days of sitting around can be too much for them. They need to work, to be busy, to earn. For others it just comes as a shock, the getting up early on a cold winter's day, the travel, the handling of frozen goods, the dictates of time. For me it was a bit of both. I had had a wonderful time but if all our dreams were to come true this year we had to both set to and earn as much as we could. On the work front the factory was ticking over. Not much fresh produce comes in in January so time was spent as before Christmas with packaging and canning. At least the canning line was warm on a cold day because it generated plenty of heat. For us in the lab this was the time for servicing the instruments that governed the work of the machines, for example the brine regulator on the pea grader. Steve was better than me at such things and he showed me how to take it apart and clean each part in carbon tetrachloride avoiding the danger of breathing in the fumes and becoming a solvent addict. Then there was stock taking in the freezer cage, not a pleasant job but a necessary one, sending replacement cans to complainants, tidying up the pump house, checking the pollution levels at the sewage farm and whatever else Tosh found for us to do. There was no overtime for the floor workers, just basic hours so both Josie and I were on basic wage. I was now on £13 a week, Josie on £6, out of which we managed to save £7 a week after giving our separate parents money for keep. We now had accrued around £50 with the £20 from Josie's parents. Would this be enough for a wedding? We had no idea but were determined to keep saving.

It was on one of these mornings that on arrival at work, a strange vehicle appeared. It looked like a glass ball on three legs and it pulled up at the factory entrance. Then just as one expects an alien to come out of a space ship the whole front opened up and out stepped Steve. It was suitably named a bubble car because of its shape and all glass surround and in keeping with its name it was joked that they were cheap to run because they ran on soap and water. It's often said that small people like big cars and large people like small cars. Well Steve was big and it did seem a little incongruous to see him step out of such a small vehicle. We all gathered around to have a good look. Some had never seen one before. You could drive one of these on a motorcycle licence and of course they had the added advantage of being both dry and warm, which a motor cycle did not. There was much interest shown and a debate as to whether it should be parked with the bikes or the cars.

Three wheels are safer than two and I was beginning to realise just how vulnerable scooters were in icy conditions. Scooters tend to have their weight lower down than motorbikes i.e. the centre of gravity is lower therefore one would think they are more stable, and they probably are but the small, wider tyres proved to be more liable to skid on ice. It was on a January night that the accident happened.

Josie and I were invited to a friend's party on a Saturday night. They were her friends, recently married, called Kevin and Irene. It was a clear evening and dry when we went to their house in a village called Tunstead just a couple of miles away. There were other friends there and Josie knew most of them. Two of them I knew from work. We had a great time. It was how parties used to be, not standing around all evening with a glass or bottle in your hand trying to make conversation over loud music. No, we played games, party games, where people made fools of themselves and everyone had a great time. One game in particular I remember required two couples to go outside the room and wait till they were asked back in. They picked on us. As an engaged couple it was fitting they said. Another couple were chosen and we four left the room. Nobody told us the name of the game. In fact they told us nothing. Then when we were out of earshot our hosts told the other guests that the game was called 'Honeymoon Night' and this was our honeymoon and how we reacted when we came back in was to be seen in that light. Nobody was to say a word. We were the first two to be brought back in and sat in front of everyone else. We sat. We waited. Nobody spoke. One or two smiled. I said "Would somebody tell us what we've got to do?" This brought the house down. I looked at Josie. She looked at me. "Do you know what we're supposed to do?" I asked her. By now the other guests were doubling up. And when Josie said "I haven't a clue" they simply roared. We were really perplexed. What had we done to make them laugh so much? Their laughter was infectious and we began to laugh, though not knowing why, and when Josie said "Well if you won't tell us what to do, how can we do it" and that brought the laughter to a crescendo and our hosts took pity on us and explained that everything we had said was seen as our utterances on our wedding night which immediately made us try to recall just what we had said, and needless to say we joined in the laughter. Then it was our turn to join the others and watch as the other poor couple was put through the same ordeal. It was a great party with similar daft but enjoyable games but at 11.30p.m. we all began to leave. When we stepped outside we realised that a frost had already set in and the pavements were slippery. However we were well wrapped up and the scooter started after the second try. We waved goodbye to Kevin and Irene and set off.

Country roads are notorious for their bends and this piece of road was no different. I wasn't going fast and didn't anticipate any trouble but all of a sudden whilst negotiating a bend I felt the scooter go. It skidded right across the road on it's side, leaving us sliding along behind it. I picked myself up and hurried to Josie who was doing the same. Luckily there was no other traffic, otherwise things might have been worse but when we looked, neither of us had suffered more than a slight bruise. Fortunately the ice had coated the road surface so where we might have sustained cuts and scrapes we had simply slid. Naturally we were shook up and I picked the scooter up. The engine was still running and as far as I could see was still all-intact. We had no choice but to remount and set off, only this time I went even slower with my feet dangling just above the road surface so I could use them as stabilisers if needed. Fortunately we made it with no other mishaps and we had already planned that I would stay the night so I didn't need to face the road again. But I was very wary for the rest of the Winter especially when I had Josie with me.

Things were happening in the corridors of power at the factory of which we were not aware. Discussions were held and decisions made and papers signed and finally it became common knowledge. We had been taken over. The new owners were Ross Foods Ltd. and we were to become Ross Foods{Westwick} Ltd. As far as we were all concerned it made no difference at all. Nobody was sacked or made redundant. The management structure remained exactly the same. One new man arrived however, from somewhere. His name was Karl, English but of European origin. He was a 'Time and Motion' man and we joked that he seemed to have lots of time and little motion. He was a friendly, slim man in his thirties and he brought no threat to us. He made his base in the lab and wandered about the factory with clipboard and pen. He obviously made reports to someone though I wasn't aware of any great changes.

One of the tasks for us in the lab was to experiment with better ways of doing things. For example, no one had ever satisfactorily canned cauliflower. As every housewife knows, one of the smells that tends to remain in the kitchen is the smell of greens cooking and nobody wants to produce a canned product that competes with that smell when opened. Nobody would buy it, or at least they wouldn't buy it twice and our business depended on repeat purchases. That was the smell we got when we opened the cans we experimented on. As well as that, cauliflower should look white when cooked. These looked yellow. Certain products we know react with the metal of the cans used and for that reason there are different lacquers on the inside of cans for different contents. We tried them all, to no avail, the result was the same. Then we tried a substance called cyclamate, a synthetic sweetener, but that failed too. In the end the experiments were abandoned. At this time competition was very intense between frozen food factories and new products were eagerly sort. Bird's Eye was one of our competitors and it was even feared that some would spy on others for the latest secrets.

I have always been amazed at some of the foods that can now be bought as frozen meals, such as bread and butter pudding and bubble and squeak, meals that were so easy to make and used up left over food. Why would anyone want to buy them? The same is true of something that Karl experimented on: Welsh Rarebit. Somebody decided that it could be canned. There were additives of course but basically it was cheese. To the uninitiated it's just cheese on toast. Karl's job was to see if the preparation of it would be economical. Large cheeses arrived at the lab and our lab ladies set to work cutting one up in small pieces before they were placed in an industrial mixer with big steel blades, to be turned into paste. But this wasn't good enough for Karl, there had to be a better way. He suggested putting the whole round cheese in the mixture, measuring 15 inches diameter and weighing several pounds, and letting the mixer do the work. Everybody said it couldn't be done. It would jam up the machine. It would break the blades. But Karl had to try, and he did, and to everybody's amazement it worked, cutting out the need to chop it up by hand. Where this all led to I don't know. We never manufactured it. I don't know if others did.

Weddings of course need planning and ours depended on us finding accommodation. We spoke to people, checked shop windows for adverts, and looked in the local paper but to no avail. People were sympathetic, said they'd keep their eyes open, but were unable to help. Then we saw an advert in the district paper for several flats just completed at a place called Hanworth. I didn't know where this was but it turned out to be a little village about 5 or 6 miles to the north west of North

Walsham. It seemed a long way to me but our curiosity got the better of us and we phoned and asked for details. It wasn't ideal but nothing else had come up so we went. It was a Saturday morning. We followed the agent's directions and eventually found it. It looked like a large country house, a vicarage or something, set in its own grounds. Surely this couldn't be it. We looked again at the address. Yes, this was it. We rode up the drive. The front door was open so we knocked and went in. The house had been converted into several self contained flats and they were beautiful. Each had a living space, kitchen/diner, bedroom and bathroom, completely redesigned and refurbished plus there was access to a walled garden in which each tenant could grow his own vegetables. It was perfect. It was all that we desired. We longed to have one, but then reality clicked in. Firstly they were £4 a week; secondly a decision needed to be made now or very soon, which meant paying a rent well before we needed it; and thirdly, was it a practical place for us both to live, especially when we might be working different shifts. We went outside to discuss it and I laid all these oppositions before Josie. I think she had come to the same decision. "I'm sorry love" I said "but we can't do it"

"I know" she said sadly "but it would have been lovely."

"I know. But we'll find something. I promise. Something will turn up." Reluctantly, we set off. On reflection it might not have been the best thing to do to go there but it gave us an idea of what to expect. Also, I never said it but we had talked about having children and were both very keen. What if she became pregnant living there, could we still afford it and how lonely she would be when I was doing long shifts. No, all in all we made the right decision.

Chapter 16

It was in February that tragedy struck the village. Fiona, Josie's mum, answered a knock on the door. It was a neighbour to tell her that there had been an accident at Bates' farm. Bates' farm was where Peter her husband worked. The caller had no other details other than that an ambulance and fire engine were on the scene. Fiona immediately panicked, as did Melanie who was also there and highly pregnant. The neighbour offered to take them there in his car and as quickly as they could they got into the car and drove off. Fiona had wanted Melanie to stay but she had refused. They arrived at the farm and it was clear that something had happened by the people milling round and the emergency services there. The police were also there and trying to keep people back. Fiona was the first out of the car and not waiting for Melanie she dashed forward to see what had happened and to find Peter. She feared the worse and reaching the police cordon frantically scanned the scene. She couldn't see her husband anywhere. There was no fire, but fire and ambulance men were crouched round a farm tractor. It was one of those with two long extending spray arms that could be folded up when not needed and opened up for maximum width when spraying the fields. Fiona couldn't wait any longer and breaking through the cordon she made for the crowd of men. As she got there she saw the familiar jacket her husband wore and cried out his name. The jacket rose and turned round and Peter came to her.

"Oh Peter" she cried as she fell into his arms "I thought something had happened to you."

"There, there lass" he said comforting her "I'm alright. It's not me. I'm not hurt."

"But who is it? What's happened?"

"It's Tom" he said gravely "He's had an accident."

"But what's happened? Is he all right?"

"I'm afraid not. He's been electrocuted. The ambulance men are with him now but there doesn't seem much hope."

"Electrocuted? But how?"

"Overhead cables. Apparently the arms of the sprayer touched them. He's been told about them so many times he should have lowered the arms...he should have lowered the arms." Just then Melanie arrived, having persuaded the police she had a right to be there and in deference to her condition they let her through. Peter saw her first. "Take her away!" he said to Fiona "Don't let her near here!" and Fiona put her arm around her and led her away. A few moments later a pitiful cry was heard from the direction they had gone and it was clear that Melanie had been told. Peter was right. Tom had not survived the shock, and he was driven away in the ambulance whilst the firemen made the scene safe and the police dispersed the crowd. It was a sombre crowd that returned to their homes that afternoon. Neighbours comforted Tom's mother and Peter and Fiona took Melanie home in a very distressed state. They were worried that the shock might have caused her to have an early labour so made very sure that she wasn't left alone. We only heard about it in the factory about an hour later when a delivery truck passed on the news. When Josie knew, she clocked off early to hurry home and Tosh allowed me to take her there. Although Melanie had broken with Tom for several months and seemed to be over him, this shock had hit her rather badly. Whether or not she had had any hopes of a reconciliation after the birth or not we couldn't tell. Melanie was not saying.

The funeral took place a week later. Melanie insisted on attending and Peter and Fiona accompanied her. Much of the village was there. Josie chose not to go, saying that whilst she felt sorry for his family she had never liked him and it would be hypocritical of her to attend. An enquiry was held into the accident to which Peter had to report. The verdict of 'accidental death' was given but several recommendations for safety were made. The village returned to a semblance of normality.

Part 2

Chapter 17

Early March 1962- It was now a year since I first arrived at Westwick; that interview which was to change my life. I had learnt new skills, made new friends and found the girl of my dreams. If a man can ever claim contentment, I was that man. I didn't claim happiness because happiness depends on circumstances. If the circumstances are good one is happy, if not, one is not happy. Contentment is different. It overrides circumstances, and doesn't depend on them. Happiness is the icing on the cake, and I was about to get a great slab of icing.

The time for Melanie's delivery was only two weeks away. Her sadness over Tom was only occasionally visible, with a word or a place to remind her. She had brought a crumb of comfort to Tom's mother by visiting her and telling her that she was bearing Tom's child and that she wouldn't be excluded from her grandchild. She left her with tears of gratitude. Josie and Fiona were as excited as Melanie was and every preparation that could be made was being made.

On the home front we were no further forward, at least that's what we thought. Unknown to us however Tosh had been working on our behalf and he took me aside one morning and said that he had made enquiries about houses the Estate owned and apparently one had become vacant and was I interested. 'Was I? Of course I was" I said "Where is it?"

"Just up the road, in Westwick. It's called Old Hall Farm. It's the old farm house. It's been turned into two houses, renovated apparently. Do you want to see it?" I couldn't wait, so Tosh left Steve in charge and borrowing one of the firm's cars he drove me there. It took us about 5 minutes. It was out to the North Walsham Rd. turn right and head for the Arch. The farmhouse was on the right opposite two small bungalows. No other houses were near it. It was a tall imposing building set at right angles to the road with a curving drive leading up to the front door, but we didn't go up the drive, instead we pulled up on the land to the left of the drive. We were now looking at the side of the house for the house was built in the shape of the letter 'L' and it was at the corner that the house had been split into two separate dwellings.

"That's the house" he said and I looked. It was very tall and appeared to have four levels because I could see windows at four levels. The front door was up a flight of steps facing the road. We walked around to the left. There was the back door and I wondered if that was the original backdoor to the farmhouse proper. Past the backdoor we walked into a typical farm yard which was surrounded on three sides by cattle sheds which had long since seen or heard the sound of cattle. We returned to the front. From the house to the road was a huge expanse of garden which hadn't been cultivated in years and was already sprouting blackthorn amongst the perennial weeds.

"This is obviously the garden" said Tosh "and by the look of those weeds it'll grow anything. So what do you think?"

"What do I think? It's amazing. It's just what we've been looking for. No! It's far better than what I imagined we'd ever get, but can we afford it? How much is it?"

"Well that's up to Mr. Alexander. It's his property. We'll have to go and see him. We might as well do that now. If he's in we can get it settled" I still didn't believe this was happening. After all the trouble we'd had finding a place and now here on our doorstep so to speak was the house of our dreams. We got back in the car and drove on through Westwick Arch along the road a way till we entered the gate that led to the Hall. The hall wasn't visible from the road and I confess to not being very observant as I was still in a state of shock about what I hoped would happen, though after seeing the price of the Hanworth flat I reckoned this would be at least that, or more. We arrived at the hall and Tosh ascertained whether the Chairman was in and could he see us. The answer was 'Yes' and we were led into his office. Mr Alexander was a man of few words but Tosh was on first named terms with him and after initial greetings I was introduced to him and we shook hands. It was clear from the conversation that they had both spoken previously about me and this was just a formality, a courtesy to him that I should come personally. The house was available whenever I wanted it, rent to commence on moving in. "So how much is the rent?" Tosh asked for me. He shrugged his shoulders, gave a shake of his head and said.

"Oh..£30"

"£30?" that was more than the flat cost. I looked at Tosh. He grinned at me. "That's per annum" he said. I couldn't believe my ears. A quick calculation made that 15 shillings a week, less than a pound a week.

"Alright?" Mr. Alexander said rising from his seat. Tosh looked at me. "Oh yes. Thank you very much. That's terrific" I don't think I bent down and kissed his feet but I would have if he'd wanted it. I'd have polished his shoes too afterwards. I couldn't believe my luck. I couldn't wait to tell Josie. We said our goodbyes and returned to the factory. I repeated my gratitude to Tosh several times knowing that I owed it all to him. As we got out of the car he said "I think you'd better tell someone the good news" I knew exactly what he meant and set off to find Josie. I found her at the far end of the factory in a packing line of frozen raspberries and it was clear I couldn't speak to her here so as it was nearly lunch time I told her to call at the lab on her way to the canteen because I had some news to tell her.

"Tell me now" she said.

"No. I'll tell you then" and I left her wondering what it was. Half an hour later she was there and I told her in as much detail as I could what had happened. Like me she couldn't believe it was true, especially about the rent.

"Oh John It's wonderful news. Now we can get married" and she threw her arms round me and hugged me tight. And we heard the voice of Christine saying.

"You've got all your lifetime to do that. You've only got a half an hour for your lunch. Get a move on."

What a relief it was to us that we hadn't committed ourselves to renting that flat at Hanworth. We now had no need to worry about rent at all and all of our savings could go to the wedding. Josie couldn't wait to tell her family the good news, which we did after work. They were delighted and couldn't believe it either, and I think her mother in particular thought that I must be highly thought of at work to be so lucky and at least her daughter wasn't marrying someone with no future. They gave us their blessing to go ahead with the wedding which we said we would like to take place in May before the busy season began in June. Otherwise I might not be able to get away for a honeymoon. This they agreed to and we spent that evening discussing all that this entailed. Priority was the venue of the wedding itself. Josie had her own ideas about that, a white wedding at Worstead church, which suited me fine. I would have married her anywhere. Fiona said that that was something which needed booking up immediately as Spring weddings were so popular and even now all of May might be already taken. This I promised to do at the first opportunity. But before any of this Josie wanted to see inside the house. She knew it's location from living so close for 19 years and Peter said that he couldn't remember when it was last lived in. He reckoned no cattle had been there for at least 30 years. He hoped it was in liveable condition. I was able to reassure them all that from looking in the windows it was clear it had been decorated throughout. Even the front and back doors were new. So as soon as I could get the keys I promised we would go and look over it thoroughly.

That became possible the very next day. Once again Tosh came to our aid, getting the keys for us, and after work we eagerly went there. There was no path from the road to the front door, only a track made by those involved in the restoration work. We parked the scooter on this path and walked up to the house. We decided to go in through the back door and the first thing we noticed was the smell of newly painted walls and ceilings. The room we entered was the living room. It was quite large with two smallish windows to the front. There was a fireplace, beside which was a cupboard. Inside we discovered it was the airing cupboard which was heated by a back boiler from the open fire. To our left was the kitchen. It was very basic with just an oven, sink and cupboard underneath. Across the living room was a door which led to the stairs. As we opened this door with an old-fashioned lift latch we saw immediately to our right another door. When I opened it I nearly fell in, for stairs led down to a cellar. I went in. There were shelves all around and a small window at ground level which let in the light. This was ideal for storing all manner of things. We closed the cellar door and proceeded up the stairs which curved to the right and brought us to the front door. On the left was a second living room, a cosy little room with a tiled fireplace set across the corner. This was the first room that had been wallpapered. Carrying on again, we went up some more stairs and came to a corridor leading off to the left. Along here was the bathroom on the left with all-new bath, toilet and handbasin. Straight ahead was the main bedroom, long but narrow, but big enough for a double bed. All rooms overlooked the front garden except for the kitchen, which overlooked the back. From the bedroom, returning, yet more stairs which took us up to the second, smaller bedroom. This too had been wallpapered. "This will make a nice nursery" I whispered to Josie and she cuddled me and gave me a knowing smile. "Well that's it" I said as we made our way down stairs again. "What do you think of it?"

"It's beautiful" she marvelled. "It couldn't be better. I can't wait for mum to see it."

"Well anytime you like now. We've got the keys. Let her see it." We went outside and I showed her the cattle yard and the garden, at least the potential garden. Then we locked up and stood out front taking in the view and trying to match each of the windows to the rooms we had seen. We surveyed the land. Apart from two huge trees at the bottom of the garden which looked like apple trees the rest was scrub, but to us it was the Promised Land.

"We'll be happy here won't we John?" she said putting her arm round me.

"We'll have a damn good try" I replied and we kissed on it.

Chapter 18

Concentrating on work was difficult now with so much going on. A trip to the vicarage to arrange the wedding venue was next on the cards. The vicar was sympathetic to our timetable and after perusing his calendar was able to offer us the 19th of May at 3pm. A glance at Josie for confirmation and she nodded agreement with a broad grin. We thanked the vicar and after agreeing to see him later to discuss matters more fully we left feeling highly elated. One more task to be ticked off as done. Would we be so lucky with booking a room for the reception? The village hall, which was just down the road, would be the obvious choice. A vicar may be able to fit many weddings in on a day but a village hall will only take one reception. We decided to give it a go. We found out who was responsible for the hall bookings, a Mrs. Marsh, and made contact with her straight away. This was our first disappointment. The hall was already booked, had been for months but she would take our names in case of cancellation.

"Is that likely?" I asked.

"With weddings, anything can happen" she answered. So we had to go with it and think of somewhere else to book.

Meanwhile in the factory, one more change as a result of the take-over. A new face appeared in the lab. And yet it wasn't a new face, at least not to me. It was a face I had last seen about ten years ago. His name was Terry Barwell and he used to be the Akela at my scout group. The last I remember seeing him was when at a jamboree he was playing the Green Eyed Yellow Idol from the town of Kathmandu and at the end of it he jumped off the stage in this horrendous mask and scared us all to death. He had now joined us for part of the week as a chemist. He was also working for Ross Chicken Ltd. at the time. It was good to renew his acquaintance again though it was a case of me remembering him rather than him remembering me. He was working on a newer, cheaper disinfectant for the use of the whole Ross group. It was good to have him with us for he was fun to be with and had a store of jokes to tell and amuse us. For instance he said you can always tell a bachelor's flat from others because all the houseplants are dead and there's something growing in the fridge. I suppose it was his kind of joke being a chemist. Then he told us about the time he took his wife out to a meal. One of the starters was tongue. She wasn't quite sure what it was so he explained it was an ox tongue.

"Oh I can't have that." she said.

"Why not?" he asked.

"Oh I couldn't eat anything that's been near a cow's mouth."

"So what are you having then?" he asked her.

"I think I'll have the oxtail soup." she said. Well true or not, it kept us amused.

Almost to the day expected, Melanie's labour began. There had been a couple of false alarms but this one proved to be the real thing. The midwife got her in to North Walsham Cottage Hospital in good time and her mum went with her. Two hours later she gave birth to a 7lb 7oz baby girl. Both mother and baby were fine. I heard about it next day at work from Josie and both were still well. She was desperate to go and see them both so I agreed to take her after work. So ascertaining visitor hours we rode there in the evening and were directed to the maternity ward. Her parents were both there already and Melanie was sitting up chatting to them, her daughter in a cot beside. We had taken the usual grapes and magazines but all eyes were on the new-born. As yet a name hadn't been finally decided but the favourite for Melanie was Cindy. Both Fiona and Josie took turns in holding her and when I saw Josie with her I must confess to a mixture of jealousy and anticipation for the day when she'd do the same with ours. We stayed for a while till time was called and then left. Arriving home before her parents, who had to catch a bus, we sat on the settee and cuddled up.

"She was lovely, wasn't she" she said.

"I take it you mean the baby" I quipped.

"Of course, the baby, but I do wonder how Melanie is going to cope on her own."

"Yes. It certainly won't be easy."

"I'm so glad I've got you John. I couldn't cope on my own in that situation."

"Well you won't have to my darling. I'm here to stay." and we made the most of our time until we heard the key in the lock and her parents entered.

Melanie was in hospital for a full ten days. It was the practice in the sixties even for natural births and she was desperate to get out. She came home to a full family celebration and a new life for everyone because the household had to adapt to it's newest member. Cindy Louise were her names and it was decided that she would bear the family name of Fisher.

Josie had decided that both Melanie and my sister Karen would be bridesmaids and I needed to choose a best man. This did create some problems and I took time to think about it. There was no male friend that I felt close to, someone who knew me well enough to carry out the role and make one of those best man speeches that are meant to be both riotous and revealing. It was Fiona who suggested Steve. She'd heard us talking about him, always complementary, and thought maybe he would be suitable. Josie and I both agreed that he would be ideal if he would do it and I agreed to ask him.

The venue for the reception still hadn't been resolved though we had made several enquiries at other village halls in the vicinity and were getting desperate. This was delaying the sending out of invitations. We had even joked about holding it at our new home and asking everyone to bring a piece of furniture. Josie was fortunate in having an aunt who was a seamstress and had agreed to make her dress and the bridesmaids' dresses as her wedding gift. Catering was to be a family prepared buffet but the cake was ordered specially as her parents' gift.

It was in the midst of all these preparations and celebrations that sadness struck the factory. Upto now you had always been able to rely on Jimmy to brighten your day, Whatever the task, if Jimmy was there, at least you knew that he would have something cheerful to say. Until one day, when his whole countenance seemed to change. He still did his work, still didn't grumble, but you could tell he wasn't the same. Something had changed him. He no longer made jokes and in the canteen, instead of sitting with the others, he took to sitting on his own. Those who tried to get near him, found that they couldn't. He wouldn't open to anyone. This continued for two or three weeks till word got out from somebody who lived near him that his wife had left him and taken his children with her to Hunstanton. When people knew, they sympathised with him, tried to empathise with him but somehow the fact that others knew depressed him even more. And then one day he wasn't there. Speculation was rife as to what had happened to him. Some were genuinely worried for him to the extent that they called at his house to see if he was alright but he wasn't there. Neighbours said they hadn't seen him lately. Others thought it a good sign that he had gone to his wife and patched things up and it was for the best.

It was two weeks later that a police car was seen at the factory office, not an unusual occurrence with so many people employed here. But this time the news wasn't good. Just past Westwick Arch and on through the estate, the road dips into a valley where there are lovely lakes right up to the road surrounded by rhododendron bushes, a lovely sight in late May. A body had been found floating there by an estate worker. It had been identified as Jimmy. Foul play had been ruled out and suicide suspected. Some of his work mates were questioned as to his state of mind and eventually the coroner brought in a verdict of 'suicide'. This sent a pall of remorse over the factory and a collection was taken for flowers for his funeral which one or two attended. Needless to say, our joy was suspended and partially extinguished for a while.

But it was reignited again when at the point of despair we had a call from Mrs. Marsh saying that there had indeed been a cancellation of the booking for May 19th and the hall was ours if we wanted it. We were of course delighted and got back to her immediately. We didn't enquire as to why the hall had become vacant we just paid our deposit and left. But I wondered afterwards just what had caused a wedding reception to be called off. When one is so happy it's sad to think that another couple might have changed their minds about getting married. I hoped that they'd just found a different venue for themselves and would be just as happy as us on our wedding day. But then there was Jimmy. He obviously loved his wife and look what had happened to him. Life could be so cruel. But none of this was going to happen to us. We sent off the invitations with a feeling of relief that the last obstacle was now out of the way. I had asked Steve if he would be my best man. He said 'No' unless he could chaperone the bridesmaids as well. I said that was obligatory, so he agreed to do it. He said it would be his first time as best man. I said that it would be my first time as a bridegroom. So he reckoned we were equal.

Bit by bit we got together the basic furniture for our new home. Very little was new. We were either given it or we bought it second hand. There was a shop in Coltishall which sold just about anything for anyone, keeping a commission for items sold. We bought a chaise longue, very reasonable, which we put in front of the fire in the main living room. And because the floor was wooden I bought a carpet 7ft by 5ft made of cotton to go in front of it. It cost £7 but still left a lot of floor uncovered. Lino had been put on the floor in the upstairs lounge so we put two armchairs in there. Being small it was cosier and would be easier to heat we thought. Apart from a double bed and a chest of drawers the main bedroom was bare. All of the windows were small so curtains were not a problem.

On the floors we had two or three home made readicut rugs which Josie and I had made together through the winter, sitting on her mother's settee. These were put in strategic places like beside the bed. It was not luxurious by any means but it was adequate and it was ours.

Time went quickly through April, though it didn't seem long enough for Josie's aunt who needed several fittings for the three girls to get their exact sizes for their dresses. I would usually bring Karen over from Norwich so she could go with Josie and Melanie for a measuring and fitting session. I went to Burtons for my suit. There I was measured for a charcoal grey suit which would take around three weeks to make.

As agreed earlier, arrangements were made for my parents to meet Josie's. It didn't seem right that the first time they met would be at the wedding, so on a Saturday afternoon I came with them by train to Worstead Station where we were met by Peter who had borrowed a car to pick us up and take us back to his. I introduced them all and we drove to the house for what I hoped would not be an ordeal for any of us. My parents are easy going and not given to many words so I didn't know how the conversation would flow but it seemed to be going alright after the first niceties and then they got onto the forthcoming nuptials. We left them alone as much as possible, so they could talk about us if they wished, whilst we busied ourselves making tea and sandwiches in the kitchen with the occasional ear at the door. Both families were working class so there was a rapport between them and my dad was a keen gardener so he felt at ease walking around the garden with Peter whilst the women talked about flowers and food and dresses and all that. Then we had tea and talked about anything but weddings and finally, because we were governed by train times we said our goodbyes and returned to the station where we caught the Norwich train. I thought I'd better ask so I said, "Well how was it?"

"They're very nice people" said dad.

"Yes, very nice" agreed mum. I imagined Josie's parents were saying the same thing to Josie. I smiled to myself and looked out of the carriage window to see the countryside flashing by.

In the factory at the end of April, beginning of May, the first crop was coming in. Purple sprouting broccoli which had been growing for nearly a year after its initial sowing was now producing tight purple heads and was brought in in bushel boxes. The blanchers were reheated, reset and restarted. The factory came to life from it's winter recess and hummed to the sound of machinery, the smell of steam and the chatter of women on the inspection belts whose hands knew automatically what to do whilst their minds caught up on all the local gossip, and spread a fair bit as well I shouldn't wonder.

Broccoli was steam blanched and like any of the brassica family it had it's lingering smell which permeates the cooking area, be it kitchen or factory. It was one of the least pleasant odours. Much of this kind of food was now being packed in heat sealed polythene bags such as we see in supermarkets today whereas previously it might have been packed in catering size cardboard boxes. Too much handling of frozen broccoli tends to end up as dust due to it's brittle nature when frozen. Rhubarb too was in again and Aimie who had had the accident the previous year was back working on the machine. She had returned to work as soon as she was better and was now one finger shorter and a lot wiser.

There was now no crop that I hadn't processed, and in case you think we carried all these blanching and canning times in our heads we had charts issued by the Campden Food and Drink Research Association which listed all the optimum times and temperatures for processing. Ours was the skill of obtaining those times and temperatures. For example if we found the veg. was coming off a belt too fast to be looked over properly we could slow the belt down but that meant they would be in the blancher longer and therefore cooked more so we then had to lower the temperature, conversely if they wanted it quicker we would speed up the belt and increase the temperature. It was all a case of getting the right balance. After a time we knew what temperatures to set food at but the charts were there to refer to in case of doubt and when we hadn't handled a certain crop for a year.

Unfortunately there are no charts available on the subject of weddings, no hard and fast rules, only advice, and that I got aplenty from those ladies on the inspection belt, most of whom were married, some for a long time by the look of them. I was one of the subjects of their gossip and I got lots of advice, from how to keep a wife happy, to not getting married at all, reflecting the whole spectrum of their collective experience. But with the stubbornness of youth I rejected them all, preferring to plot my own course and make my own mistakes.

Several of the people at the factory had been invited to our wedding, including Tosh and his wife, May and Phyllis. Josie had chosen her closest friends, including Christine for whom she had a lot of respect. Tosh had invited us both to tea at his house. We had not yet met his wife and now we were into May and the weather was fine he thought it suitable for us to meet. We went there on a Sunday afternoon. He had given us directions and we found our way there taking only one wrong turning. His cottage was in Dilham just east of Worstead. A small byroad, overlooked by a field and a high bank, had a row of cottages on the left of which his was one. He was there to welcome us, again wearing slacks and his favoured check shirt. He introduced us to his wife Jean and his children, 4 girls and a boy. His oldest daughter was about Josie's age and they felt they had met somewhere before, probably at school, but it gave them something to chat about. They made us feel at home with the youngest children content after the initial introductions, to play outside in the garden. We had a cup of tea and then Tosh showed me round his garden, leaving Josie to chat with Jean and her daughter. His garden was his passion. He was fully into garden management with all that that involved with recycling and composting and the results were clear to see. At the bottom of the garden were the chickens I had heard him speak affectionately of, egg laying machines for his big family. Josie got on well with Jean who was very much the caring housewife and mother.

I remember our tea consisted almost entirely of home grown salad, with hard boiled eggs and ham. And I'm sure that had it been Summer we would have had tomatoes and new potatoes from the garden too. I was greatly impressed by the notion of self sufficiency and vowed to try my best to achieve the same with the land we were to get. I think too that Tosh got pleasure from influencing others into his passion, by the almost affectionate way he spoke about the soil, and how you had to put a lot in to get a lot out. I fancied he felt the same about his family and though he loved his daughters, his youngest child, his son had completed his joy as a family man.

We left after tea, with their best wishes for our forthcoming wedding, and yes, they would be coming and were looking forward to it. We thanked them for their kindness and as I watched them all together as we said goodbye I thought that they had something we would do well to strive for ourselves, and hoped we would achieve it.

The last two weeks before the wedding were frantic. I felt sorry for the Fisher household, for on top of all they had to do, they were suffering disturbed nights from Cindy Louise. Melanie was desperately trying to get her figure back to fit into the bridesmaid dress, Josie was beginning to panic about just anything, Fiona was trying to keep everybody calm, and Peter thought it wise to absent himself when ever possible. I gave moral support wherever possible and tried to correlate the invitation replies with numbers of places required in the hall. We had our talk with the vicar who impressed on us the importance of what we were doing and the sanctity of marriage. We assured him of our sincerity and we talked about the order of service and the hymns we had chosen which seemed to satisfy him. Bans were being read out for the required number of weeks before the date and we attended one of those services to hear them. It was a beautiful church though sadly lacking those stained glass windows that so lift one's spirits at their beauty and colour, and the pews were still the enclosed family pews which gave the look of antiquity about them, but we were proud to join the myriad of others who had gone before us and made their vows over the centuries.

I had booked our honeymoon with a travel agent but had refused to tell Josie where we were going, wanting it to be a surprise. But I assured her it wasn't Mundesley or Happisburgh but we would need to catch a train to Norwich and then another from there. This I had to disclose because of the logistics of time and travel. I assured her there would be no other secrets in our marriage, apart from birthdays and Christmas that is. There were however secrets all around us. May and Phyllis had been furtively canvassing everybody in the factory for a donation for a wedding present from the factory as a whole and they had to do it when we weren't around. They were very persuasive people and I couldn't help noticing the times when I came into the lab were the times when they went out.

The week of the wedding was perhaps less stressful as most things that could be done were done. This did not however take away that awful dread that on the day something might have been overlooked, something, like the flowers wouldn't turn up, or the wedding car would go to the wrong address. But you just had to wait and hope. Because there was so much to do on the Friday, Josie had decided to have that day off. Fortunately they knew that in advance at the factory and as she was about to leave off and was saying goodbye to her friends, who were wishing her all the best, Christine came along and told her she was wanted at the lab. I was already there and knew nothing of this until she arrived. Then it was apparent that something was happening because several other people arrived and as we were placed side by side Tosh came forward and made a speech on behalf of everybody wishing us both, long life and happiness and as a token of their affection gave us a gift from all our friends at the factory. It was big, in wedding paper wrapping and Josie was to open it. This she did tentatively, with encouragement from the onlookers, to reveal a box which clearly stated the contents were a dinner service. Together we opened the box to admire the array of plates and dishes etc. with a lovely country scene emblazoned upon them. Josie was speechless and a little tearful so I thanked everybody on her behalf and said somebody must have seen our present list because we certainly never had anything as lovely as this. After more best wishes Josie left. I wouldn't see her again till we arrived at the church so in the privacy of the room at the end of the lab we said our goodbyes with a hug and a kiss and she left for home.

I had one more day's work to do before a week away. It seemed a long day. I knew that others were working hard to make tomorrow a special day. I wished I could be there to help them. All I had to do was make sure that Steve would be there. Conversely he had to make sure I would be. In our less busy moments we compared notes and agreed that we were both on course. He had written a speech and was generally pleased with it.

"Will it be the truth though?" I asked him.

"Who cares?" he laughed. "It'll be a giggle."

"But you're supposed to tell them about me." I argued.

"Oh I'll do that" he grinned "Don't you worry."

Now I began to worry, knowing his love of a good joke, anything could happen. Karen was due to come over from Norwich sometime today and spend the night at Josie's so that she would be there for the morning. Josie was having a small gathering of girl friends that evening for a sort of hen party but I decided against the equivalent male stag party as I'm not a drinker and I needed all my wits about me for the next day. Josie assured me she wouldn't get drunk either. She too wanted to look her best on the day. My brother was going to take me to Steve's house in Hoveton the next day and we'd travel to church together. My family had hired a mini-bus to bring them all from home, others would make their own way there. All these thoughts were going through my head as I switched on blanchers, started up canning lines, and listened to ribald remarks from the factory floor such as "Where are you spending your honeymoon then John?" answered by someone else "In bed of course" or "Doing anything interesting tomorrow night then John?" I'd heard them all by the end of the day and took it all in good humour. At the end of the day I was glad to say my farewells, knowing I'd see many of them again tomorrow, and I headed for home.

Chapter 19

May 19th was a warm sunny day. I awoke to the knowledge that I was about to embark on what was probably the most important day of my life, and the butterflies were already taking off. I knew Josie, Melanie and Karen were expecting a visit from a hairdresser that morning. I had to do my own. I prided myself on my Brylcreemed black hair and I probably spent as much time on it as they would on theirs, but then I had all morning. Four things I needed to take with me: my suitcase for going away, the tickets for the journey, button holes for Steve and me, and of course the ring. I had little appetite for food but mum made me eat a bit of toast.

"We don't want you passing out at the altar do we" she said.

"*Oh god!*" I thought, "*not in front of all those people.*"

My brother Keith arrived at 1.30pm and now arrayed in my Burton's suit we set off. It was early but I preferred that to arriving late. And anyway, '*what if the car broke down or there was a traffic jam?*' You never knew. We picked up Steve around 2pm and I introduced him to my brother Keith. Steve looked very smart in a grey suit and shiny black shoes and I realised I'd never seen him before without his welly boots. We finally arrived at the church at about 2.20 and decided that we were too early and we should stay in the car for a while. There were people outside the church but we could see nobody we knew and then we realised they were waiting for another wedding which was just concluding.

"It's not too late to change your mind" quipped Steve with a cheeky grin.

"Not likely" I replied "I've never been so sure of anything in my life."

"I'm glad to hear it" said Keith sounding relieved.

The bride and groom appeared and we watched the events take place that would shortly be mine and Josie's. Then leaving Keith with the car we slipped by the revelry and entered the church. One or two stragglers were still admiring the church, which had been abundantly decorated with flowers and bouquets, a joint effort from all the day's participants. We walked down the aisle as the vicar appeared having a cup of tea, I thought he probably needed it between services. At least I presumed it was tea. He welcomed us and we had a few words and I noticed people were now coming in and sitting down. Now the butterflies were really taking off.

"Have you got the ring?" I asked Steve.

"What ring?" he asked innocently.

"Oh please?" I begged.

"Oh *that* ring?" he grinned, "Course I have. Stop worrying."

A swift glance showed lots of familiar faces offering encouraging smiles. Then my family appeared and took their seats, followed by Josie's mum. There was a murmur of conversation all around and then an expectant hush and only then did it really hit me that it was about to happen. I sat down, took a deep breath and waited. How I wished I'd ate more toast.

It was the wedding march that brought me and everyone else to our feet, and I dared not look back for fear of the sea of faces I would encounter, but I needn't have worried for all eyes were on Josie, and after what seemed like an interminable wait it became obvious why, as she eventually came into my line of vision on her father's arm and I saw her, the most beautiful creature in white, wearing a figure hugging brocade dress embossed with lillies of the valley and carrying a bouquet of yellow roses. I moved beside her as her proud but relieved father relinquished her to me. I looked into her eyes and was once again mesmerised by her beauty and as we exchanged smiles I whispered "You're beautiful."

I don't remember much of the service. It went as planned and Steve did the ring bit. We both said what we were supposed to say and the vicar pronounced us man and wife and I got to kiss my darling wife. No man could have been happier. The butterflies had gone and I noticed for the first time the two lovely bridesmaids Melanie and Karen in long pale blue dresses. I was aware that Steve noticed them too as we signed the register, before walking the gauntlet back through the church to the acknowledgement of friends and family. Some were strangers to one of us but known to the other, the wider family, who got brought together on such occasions, and who we'd probably never see again till the next occasion. Outside there seemed to be more people than there were in the church and more familiar faces from work were in the crowd. The photo sessions took place and for those few that didn't require me I could only stand and admire the lovely girl who was now my wife.

In the end we had to vacate the churchyard for yet another happy couple who were waiting to enter and we all made our way to the village hall to the left of the church about 50 yards down School Road on the right This was when Steve came into his own. He was a natural organiser and ushered all the invited guests along, though I noticed he was never far from the two bridesmaids in whom he took a special interest, and they in their turn were only too happy for his attention.

We had to be first at the hall to be greeted by the guests as they entered. The hall had been decorated with even more flowers and a marvellous spread of food was down a middle table with, at it's centre a beautiful three tiered cake topped with a bride and groom. Chairs were placed around the outside of the hall to sit on. Someone had really been busy. There was the handshaking and the kissing and the giving of presents and of course the introductions. Tosh and Jean were there, Christine, May and Phyllis and others Josie had invited and when all were in they were invited to help themselves to the food.

This should have given us some respite but there were so many people to talk to and who wanted to talk to us that we never had a moment to ourselves. Steve was doing his bit, encouraging people to partake of the food and helped with the serving of drinks. Christine came up to him and slapped him on the back saying he'd done a good job so far, for which he thanked her but he didn't realise that she'd actually stuck a card on his back which read '*Is this the best man you could find?*' and when people began to laugh as he passed by it took him sometime to realise they were laughing at him. When eventually someone took pity on him and told him about the label and he read it, he knew immediately who was responsible. He looked for Christine and seeing her, she said laughing "I told you I'd get you back" and everybody saw the joke including Steve who said "Just you wait".

Around 4.30pm came the formalities of the speeches and Steve took over. He'd obviously researched his role because he knew what to do and started by asking Peter to speak. He was a man of few words and after extolling his daughter's beauty and wishing us all the best, he sat down. I was next and endorsed what Peter had said about Josie and proceeded to thank everybody for coming and for all their gifts and for all that they had done to make this such a happy day, especially Fiona, Josie's mum who had supervised the hall arrangements and much more. Then came Steve's turn. I had dreaded what he might say, but he seemed quite at ease, which worried me even more. He started by holding a piece of folded paper and saying he'd just jotted down a few notes, then he let go of one end of the paper and it unfolded and fell, till it reached the floor, which immediately got everybody laughing and in a good mood for the rest of his speech. He said a lot of things about me, mostly made up, but intended to amuse, most of which I forget but I remember the first thing he said. It went like this "First I want to give you the honeymoon weather forecast 'Two warm fronts converging, followed by a little sun {son}'". He gave us time to digest this for some were slower than others, but it got everybody laughing. And at the end of his speech he turned to me and said "And finally John I don't want to worry you but somebody just gave Josie two aspirin" and with that he finished his speech to much applause and laughter. I found it hard to believe he'd never been Best Man before. He was a natural. There followed the proposing of the toast and then the cake was cut, which Josie and I did under the direction of the photographer.

We were now cutting it fine for our train connections, so Josie had to be driven home to change and get her luggage. Steve assured me that he was well able to look after things when we'd gone and I believed him and entrusted everything into his care. I knew that there were many trusty helpers to aid him. Shortly after, Josie returned looking serene in a pale blue suit and together we said our good byes to everyone, but just before we left Josie threw her bouquet and to everybody's surprise and delight it was caught by Melanie. Then we were showered with confetti as we hurried to Keith who was waiting in the car to drive us to the station. So with a last wave and goodbye we finally left.

On the train it was hard to disguise the fact that we were newly wed. Even without the confetti which we had tried to eliminate from our hair and clothes without success our very aura of happiness would have given us away and I realised after two stations that I still had my carnation in my buttonhole. We changed trains at Norwich and were able to relax with a long journey to London ahead of us.

"So now you can tell me where we're going" Josie said snuggling up close.

"We're on our way to London" I smiled at her.

"Yes I know that, but is that where we're staying?"

"No! Well we are for one night, yes. Then tomorrow we're going somewhere else."

"Right. Where?"

"I'll tell you tomorrow."

"Oh John you are awful. Why can't you tell me now?"

"Because it will spoil the surprise. Tomorrow you'll know everything... but I'll tell you one thing."

"What's that?"

"I'm starving."

"So am I. Didn't you eat anything?"

"Not a thing. I was too nervous to eat."

"Me too. All that food. I could do with it now."

"We'll eat when we get to London, Promise."
London Liverpool St.Station was where we left the train and I hailed a taxi. I gave the address to the driver and we set off. I've heard London taxi drivers are a bit scary and ours was no exception as he wove in and out of the traffic but one manoeuvre proved too daring and there was a bump and a brake and we stopped. The driver got out and we heard a confrontation with another driver. Then this other irate driver looked into our cab and shouted that we were witnesses. "You saw what happened surely."

"Sorry!" I replied "We're emigrating tomorrow we won't even be here." Eventually the taxi driver returned leaving the other driver still ranting and we carried on.

"You were joking weren't you" said Josie sounding a little worried.

"Cause I was" I laughed, "but the last thing I want to do on my honeymoon is get involved in legal disputes." We finally arrived at our destination, a huge hotel called Mount Pleasant and I paid the driver with a tip. "All the best on your journey" he said and drove off. I don't know if he meant journey abroad or the journey of life but I didn't enlighten him. We entered the hotel. It was indeed a big place and we approached the desk.

"Mr. and Mrs. Clark." I said handing a booking form to the clerk, a middle aged man with a moustache in a black suit. Josie was grinning at the mention of her new name and I suddenly realised that Clark is just one step up from Mr. and Mrs. Smith used so often for illicit affairs in hotels. By the look we were given, the clerk thought so too. Everything was in order however and a steward was called to show us to our room. He carried our two bags and we followed him to the lift and we were transported up two floors. Following him along a corridor he stopped at a room opened the door and led us in. There, he put on the lights, put down our bags, wished us a happy stay and left. My first response as I looked around the room was "No! This will never do. This is not what I asked for." For I had booked a double room and they had given us twin beds. I had waited a long time for this night and it was not going to be spoilt by this arrangement. "Don't worry Josie" I said "I'll sort it out. You stay here. I'll be back soon" Hastily I retraced our steps back to the clerk at the desk where I made my objections quite clear.

"This is my honeymoon for goodness sake. I ordered a double room and that is what I want" The clerk saw that I meant business and checking his room list, apologised profusely, called the steward over, gave him another key and sent us off again. We arrived at the first room and the steward knocked on the door, entered, picked up our bags, said "Follow me madam, sir." and led us off again. Josie was finding it all very amusing whilst I was still angry about it. But my humour returned, as passing a man in a dressing gown on a hotel telephone we heard him say he'd locked himself out of his room and could someone please help. We suppressed a smirk till we were past him then broke into laughter. We arrived at the new room and a quick look showed it to be as ordered. We thanked the man and closed the door. Then we hugged and kissed and said "We've made it."

We decided to unpack our cases for the things we would need that night and in the morning and then go for something to eat. It was then I discovered that I had forgotten my razor.

"Does it matter that much?"asked Josie "you can get another tomorrow."

"Tomorrow's Sunday, and anyway I can't go down to breakfast unshaven on my honeymoon." So we decided to ask at the reception desk if there was anywhere I could buy a razor.

"There's a late night chemist at Leicester Square" the clerk advised and told us how to get there. It wasn't far and we found it alright. Daylight was almost gone and the lights of Leicester Square dispelled the coming darkness. People seemed unaware of the now cooling evening and milled around with no apparent purpose but the pursuit of pleasure. Josie had never been here before and was enthralled by the bustle and noise, the glitz of the theatres, the lights and the people out for an enjoyable evening and it felt as if they were all participating in our wedding joy. We found the chemist and I purchased my razor. We also found a restaurant and by now we were both starving, having eaten hardly anything all day. "We must keep our strength up" grinned Josie, so we both ordered a mixed grill, even though it was late evening, and we ate every bit, and food never tasted so good. But the day had taken its toll. We were both exhausted and excited. It was our wedding night after all and hand in hand we made our way back to the hotel.

I think honeymoons were designed to turn virgins into veterans. Of course for those who live together before marriage the honeymoon is just a refresher course. That wasn't the case with us. We were ready for the induction course. So, finding an appropriate sign in our room, we hung it on the outside doorknob and closed the door. It read '**DO NOT DISTURB.**'

Dawn broke on the next day, the Sunday, and after eating a good breakfast we got another taxi to Waterloo Station. Josie was still anxious to know where we were off to so I told her. "We're spending the rest of the week in Torquay"

"Torquay?....That's in..."

"Devon" I prompted her. "the Riviera of the Devon coast. You'll love it there. I was there in 1955 and I always thought I'd like to spend my honeymoon there and now we shall."

"It sounds lovely" Josie said "Better than that, it sounds perfect."

And perfect it was in every way but one. Our hotel was comfortable enough but there was never a choice of menu and the food portions were meagre. I think they thought we were living on love and they could profit from it. So each day we had to supplement our diet from one or other of the fast food outlets. During the week we visited many places including Paignton Zoo, Dartmoor, the lovely villages of Cockington and Widecombe-in-the-Moor and had a boat trip up the River Dart where we saw Agatha Christie's house set up high in the woods.

Frozen In Time

But inevitably the time went too fast and we had to return to the world of work and reality. At the time this had no fears for us for there was much excitement still, about our new home and life together and it wasn't so much the end of a honeymoon but the continuation of it as we set off for home with eagerness and great expectations.

Chapter 20

Arriving at Norwich Station we decided it was probably wiser to catch the bus home. By train our nearest station Worstead was too far to walk with two suitcases, whereas the bus stopped right outside our house. So this we did and arrived home late in the afternoon. There were lots of practical things we had to do when we got back. We needed food for a start. Holiday clothes would need washing. That required hot water and soap powder and I needed to fetch my Lambretta from my parents' house. But on the upside we still had many presents to open. Unlocking the back door I did the traditional thing and carried Josie over the threshold, much to her amusement, and as I put her down a lovely surprise awaited us. Someone had already been there and the house smelt of fresh cleaning. There were flowers in vases and in the kitchen was a large cardboard box full of the very groceries we had been planning to get. And on the chaise longue were all the presents we had received still waiting to be opened.

"This is down to your mother" I said and then added jokingly, "Perhaps I should have married her instead of you."

"Somehow I don't think that would have been possible" she replied, "Anyway you don't know what I'm good at yet."

"Oh yes I do." I replied advancing on her.

"Oh dear what have I said now?" she giggled as she made for the stairs with me in hot pursuit. We stopped to look in the front room where again flowers were in a vase and there was the smell of polish, and then to the bedroom where we had left the bed already made for our return. We collapsed on it, and after a mock struggle I looked into her eyes and smiling said "Welcome home Mrs. Clark" and she smiling back said, "Welcome home Mr. Clark" and we kissed. But then she pushed me off her and said "Come on we've got work to do" and she left the room, and I rolled onto my back and thought *"Ah well, honeymoon's over"* and followed her downstairs.

In the early sixties, very few people had the things we take for granted today. We had no washing machine, no fridge, no telephone, and no television. Washing was done by hand, or in a boiler and wrung out through the mangle and hung out to dry. Milk was delivered each morning and there were no supermarkets. Central heating and carpets were a luxury and yet without all of these we felt like millionaires.

We enjoyed the rest of the day undoing presents and familiarising ourselves with every part of the house by filling cupboards, placing ornaments, and generally making a house into a home. By bedtime, apart from washing clothes, we had accomplished every pressing task and we went to bed feeling a real sense of achievement.

Sunday, I left early by bus to Norwich to pick up my scooter. Josie was eager to go and visit her family and we needed transport. It took me about 2 hours and I was back. Josie had done the washing and was ready to go. Her family was delighted to see us both and we each had things to tell the other. I started by thanking them for what they'd done at the house and saying how useful it was not to have to go shopping on our return. Josie told them where we'd been and made them laugh at the twin bed incident. Then she gave them a brief run down on the places we'd visited in Devon. Then it was their turn to tell us how the reception had gone after our departure. It seemed everything went well and everyone had a good meal before making his or her way home. Then Melanie interrupted to say Karen went home with her family and Steve offered to take her home which she had agreed to. And yesterday, Saturday, he had taken her out for a meal in Wroxham. So all in all it had been a good day for everyone.

"And are you seeing him again?" asked Josie.

"Oh I expect so" she smiled. "At least I hope so."

We renewed our acquaintance with Cindy Louise and stayed for Sunday lunch which was very nice. It was the biggest meal we'd had since Leicester Square and much appreciated.

In the afternoon we said our goodbyes as neither of us wanted to be away from our new home for long and I rode the scooter whilst Josie rode her bike for she was bound to need it for work. But my thoughts were on Steve and Melanie. I did hope he wouldn't cause her any further upset.

Back to work on Monday, I took Josie in because we started at the same time and hopefully finished the same. The inevitable greetings met us like "Oh you do look tired" and when they discovered we'd been to the coast we were asked "Did you see the sea?" amidst further laughter. In the lab the greetings were cordial, and seeing Steve I thanked him once again for all his help, to which he replied that he'd thoroughly enjoyed himself, of which I had no doubt. Then I was brought up to date with what had happened the past week until we were interrupted by someone asking for the blancher to be set for broad beans.

"Your call John" said Tosh "get back into it." After a quick glance at the chart for blanching times I set to. Broad beans come in two colours, white and green, green is generally the most popular. I have known a whole field be rejected by the factory on the grounds of their being the wrong colour. There isn't much that needs checking with broad beans. They are a very clean crop, having come from a pod, but have to be inspected all the same. The nearest I can describe the smell of them when blanched is that of frying bacon, quite appetising till you've had hours of it then the appetite goes. Rhubarb too was in again and mushrooms which are available at anytime of the year being grown indoors and not relying on the weather. The canning line too was in full steam with the rhubarb being canned straight from the slicer. Everyone was busy and would be now for the next four months.

For two weeks Josie and I had the benefit of sharing our evenings together, knowing that this would all change with the pea harvest. During this time we made a start on the garden. I had planned to make a lawn in front of the house and Josie thought it would be nice to have rockeries at the back to make more of a border between us and the neighbours. I desperately wanted to make a clear path to the road from the back door. All were arduous tasks because of the uneven terrain and the headstart the weeds, particulary ground elder and bracken had on us, but with tools that Peter had given us we had virtually levelled out the lawn area by the end of the week, dug it over, trod it down and scattered grass seed. It felt good, even though we both felt tired at the end of each day. This was our home and we were going to make it as good as possible and whilst the evenings were warm it gave us a great deal of pleasure and satisfaction.

It seemed that Steve and Melanie were getting on well too. They had gone out together once or twice. He had of course known her when she worked at the factory but it had taken the wedding for him to notice her properly. Now that she was post natal she had thought about returning to the factory but of course it all depended on whether Fiona would look after Cindy. This Fiona agreed to do but only on the day shift and only for the present whilst Cindy was a baby. It was not a permanent arrangement. So Melanie was taken back at work as the pea harvest began, along with many others.

Once again we were into 24 hour work. Tosh did the day shift as expected. I was on from 3p.m. to midnight and Steve from 11p.m. to 8 a.m. Steve and I would change shifts in mid July. This shift of mine had its advantages and disadvantages. It meant that I had all day to work in the garden and get it sorted but it also meant that our evenings together had ceased. We would see each other at work for two hours each day and for an hour or so in the morning at home, but Josie would have to make her own way there to work and back. I was also worried about her being alone for the whole evening. There was nothing I could do about that but we hired a television to at least keep her company.

This shift arrangement also suited Melanie because she didn't work in the evenings and neither did Steve. But inevitably this led to friction in the Fisher household for having looked after Cindy all day Fiona expected Melanie to take over in the evenings. Melanie, being a seventeen year old teenager, wanted to spend time with Steve whenever possible and although Fiona accepted that Melanie needed the odd evening off it soon became clear to her that she was being taken advantage of.

Meanwhile I was doing well with the garden, or at least I thought so. I had dug an area about a yard from the cattle sheds which I had intended to use as a vegetable garden. Exploring the cattle sheds one day and kicking at the floor inside, I realised that it wasn't the floor but a six inch layer of cattle dung. It had laid there for many, many years and was bone dry. So with my spade I prised some up from the concrete floor and what I can only describe as cattle cake came up intact. It was possible to put my arms under it and lift it up. It had no smell and contained no moisture. It was perfect fertiliser. So I added this to the soil that I had dug. If the soil was as fertile as Tosh had said it was, it was now super fertile. In this I planted rows of Greyhound cabbage plants and early Snowball cauliflowers which Peter had given me. Even though it wasn't early in the year I hoped they would catch up.

I was still concerned about Josie being alone for so long in such a remote place. Another young couple occupied the front of our house. He worked for the estate, I believe, as a manager. He had a car and we were on nodding acquaintance with them but we never really got to know them. Across the road in one cottage lived a middle-aged couple with a teenage son and an old lady lived in the other but even so we were isolated. So I had an idea which I put to Josie one morning over breakfast.

"Why don't we get a dog?"

"A dog?"

"Yes, a dog. It would be company for you and if we got the right one it would protect you."

"Who from?"

"Well I don't know who from. From anybody I suppose. I just thought with all this land it would love living here and it would be company for you, well for us."

"I suppose so. Did you have one in mind?"

"Well as a matter of fact," I showed her an advert I had

Frozen In Time

seen in a magazine 'Border Collie pups for sale' "these. What do you think?" She perused it for a while then she said "Well I suppose it would be nice.....okay, let's do it."

"Leave it to me" I said "I'll send for one. Male or female?"

"I really don't mind....alright female, two girls together on long lonely nights. We'll have lots to talk about" So the decision was made and I did the necessary paper work. I know I said at the beginning that I wasn't really a dog person but I felt I was fulfilling my responsibility as a caring husband.

Now we were well into the pea harvest. The seasonal ladies were back and the Irish students were as well. There were lots of new faces and a few old ones. Kieran was back with his cheery greeting "How are yous all?" and Tosh was quick to give him his old job back. Arriving at three I took over from Tosh which gave him time to relax a bit and it was much better to be busy than not. Then when Tosh had gone home mine was the lonely vigil till Steve arrived at 11p.m. Josie would usually pop into the lab before going home and I would keep her upto date with anything happening at home. She always said that the saddest part of this arrangement was having to eat alone and not being able to cook me a meal. She didn't so much mind being alone in the evenings but of course would have preferred me to be there.

Whilst Josie got on well with Christine the charge hand, that was not the case with Melanie. The reason wasn't clear. Melanie did her work as she had before, but somehow there wasn't the rapport that Josie had with her. Christine would speak to her sharply and often give her the least pleasant jobs. So much so, that others noticed it.

"What's Christine got against you?" they asked after a while.

"I don't know" answered Melanie mystified. but now that others had noticed it she knew she wasn't imagining it. She asked Josie if she knew but she couldn't throw any light on it either.

"You're probably imagining it" she said to reassure her but made a point of watching for herself.

Josie didn't work weekends so we had that time together till I started work at 3p.m., and it was on a Saturday morning that a wooden box was delivered with two strands of wire around it. On the outside was the label 'Livestock –Handle with care'. We knew immediately what it was and hurriedly found a pair of pliers to cut the wire. We opened the box and inside was this frightened little black and white bundle shivering with fright on damp newspaper. Josie immediately said "Oh you poor darling" and gathered it up in her arms. With the result that it weed all down her front. "The poor creature's frightened" she said.

"Probably could do with a drink by the look of all that weeing she's been doing" I added. So we found a dish and put some water in it and put it down in the kitchen, then we placed her near it. She hesitated at first then cautiously put her head in the dish and began to lap it up. Fortunately we had had the foresight to buy a couple of cans of dog food, anticipating her arrival, and putting some on a plate we were pleased to see her set to and eat quite a bit of it. Josie just wanted to sit and cuddle it but we left her to wander and it was quite fascinating as she wandered about in every corner sniffing. "She's getting to know the place "said Josie.

"I think it might have another purpose" I said expectantly and I was right and just quick enough to pick her up and place her outside where she relieved herself beside the wall. She occupied quite a bit of our time that day and was soon following us everywhere, not outside of course but indoors. Fortunately she found the stairs a bit difficult so you could say she was grounded. We decided to call her Scotty for no other reason than that she was a Border Collie and the first border we could think of was Scotland. I also realised that before long I would have to put a fence across the garden, with a gate for us, because we were on a busy, fast road and wanted her to enjoy the garden.

The feud between Melanie and Christine hadn't abated and one day it came to a head when Melanie asked her angrily if she had something against single mothers. Christine was married but had no children and this question made her very angry. She denied that she was being vindictive and threatened to report Melanie. She didn't however and for a little while there was some kind of unspoken truce between them. Josie had asked me if there was anything I could do about the problem but I told her that I had no jurisdiction in staff problems unless quality of production was compromised, and hoped it would sort itself out. I did however mention it to Steve who had already had an ear bashing from Melanie but he wasn't very forthcoming about either the problem or the solution. I got the feeling he knew more than he was letting on.

Fortunately our shift patterns meant that Scotty was only alone for two hours each afternoon, and was always overjoyed to see us. She couldn't do much damage because we didn't have much furniture but we did have a few accidents and made use of rather a lot of newspaper on the floor. In just a week she was noticeably bigger and eating more and she hated being left downstairs when we went to bed but we were determined to train her properly. Unfortunately that meant that we had one or two disturbed nights.

I set to putting up a 3ft. fence with wire netting and posts, some of which I found lying about amongst the undergrowth. It took a bit longer to make the gate, but finally we had an enclosure of sorts. This meant we could leave the door open when we were in the garden and Scotty could please herself whether she came out or not. I was very keen on the garden and took pride in it's development but I soon realised that dogs make no distinction between paths and gardens and I was forced to start to cultivate the area outside the wire fence.

I now saw the pea harvest from beginning to end, for the field next to us was growing peas and when their time came the viners arrived and the peas went to the factory. I also went and was probably responsible for blanching them. Kieran was still involved in the not strenuous but boring job of recording the peas every five minutes with his little pot. He was one for the ladies and we had to keep an eye on him to make sure he wasn't skiving. I once found he was missing from his post and glancing down at his record sheet I saw he had recordings for times 15 minutes ahead so I waited and when he returned I questioned him about it.

"Well it's like this you see John. Sometimes I needs to go to the toilet do you see, and it might take more than 5minutes, so I either catch up when I come back or I rush ahead before I go. Do you see what I'm saying?" I saw and I left him to it.

Fiona was now insisting that Melanie took more responsibility for her daughter. Steve was quite fond of Cindy which pleased Fiona because anybody who took Melanie seriously would have to take Cindy into consideration, but Melanie saw her as restricting her chances of finding a partner, that is when she thought about long term relationships at all, mostly she just wanted some fun, and that seemed to be what Steve wanted too which worried Fiona because that's how she got into this situation in the first place. Neither did it help matters when at the end of her tether Fiona would say "Why can't you find a good man and settle down like your sister." This just made her more rebellious. But what really brought everything to a head was when somebody told Melanie that she had seen Steve and Christine together in North Walsham. Melanie hit the roof and was determined to have it out with Steve.

The next time he came round he knew at once that something was wrong by the look on Melanie's face. She had worked herself up for this and just waded in, "I just want the truth Steve. Were you or were you not with Christine in North Walsham last Saturday?" Steve looked troubled.

"Well, actually I was."

"I think you'd better go" said Melanie crossing to the door.

"But aren't you going to let me explain?"

"There's nothing to explain. You want to carry on with a married woman, that's up to you."

"Now wait a minute. You've got it all wrong."

"No I don't think so. In fact I see it all now. No wonder she's been so nasty to me. She's jealous of us. She wants you all to her self. Well she can have you. I'm not sharing you either. Get out!" and she opened the door.

"But you've got it all wrong. I was just helping her out" Melanie laughed. "That's one way of putting it-Out!" and she pushed him out and slammed the door. Just then Fiona came in from the garden and asked.

"Whatever is all the shouting about?" as Melanie ran upstairs crying. "Oh god, not again" anguished Fiona.

Melanie wasn't at work the next day. Word was that she was ill. Josie said she'd call in and see her after work. I thought no more about it till Steve came on shift. "Did you know Melanie was ill?" I asked him.

"No I didn't", he sounded worried "What's the matter with her?"

"No idea. I thought you might know."

"Yes. I think I do" Then he told me what had happened.

"Oh no!" I groaned "No wonder she's upset. So why are you getting involved with Christine. Unless of course you prefer her to Melanie."

"No I'm not getting involved with Christine and no I don't prefer her to Melanie."

"I don't understand."

"Neither does Melanie. She wouldn't let me explain. The reason I was with Christine on Saturday was because it's her husband's birthday soon and he's into motor bikes. She'd seen this bike gear advertised cheaply and because I know something about bikes and gear she asked me to go with her to check if it was worth what they were asking. That's it. That's the truth."

"So why didn't you tell Melanie what you were doing?"

"Because her and Christine haven't been hitting it off lately and she would have objected."

"I can see that. So why didn't you explain yesterday?"

"I told you. She wouldn't let me. She shoved me out of the door. I can see how it must have looked but really it was all very innocent. I was just helping out a mate."

"So where do you want to go from here?"

"I want to explain to Melanie."

"And then?"

"I want us to be as we were."

"I see" I thought about it, "You know, I think what you need is to meet on neutral ground. What if Josie can persuade Melanie to come round to ours tomorrow evening, on some pretence or other, could you make it?"

"Course I could."

"I'm not promising anything, you realise. She may not listen to you. She may not even come around."

"I'll take that chance."

"Good. Incidentally?"

"Yes."

"Why do you think Christine's been so hard on Melanie?"

"I think it's this baby thing. Christine and her husband want to start a family and it isn't happening for them and then she sees young girls like Melanie having them so easily. It's a bit galling for her, so she takes it out on her."

"Right. Shame. Life's a bitch sometimes, isn't it? Shall we say 8 o'clock tomorrow? I'll be here of course. Good luck."

"Right, and thanks." I filled him in on what was happening in the factory, which machines were working, then left him to it and headed for home, thankful that Josie and I didn't have such problems.

It was too late to bother Josie with all this now. She seldom waited up for me. I just climbed into bed, cuddled up, told her I loved her, to which she mumbled the same and promptly returned to sleep. In the morning I explained everything to her, She had seen Melanie the previous evening so knew her side of the story and admitted that she was both angry and upset, but would do her best to get her round that evening. I wished her luck and she set off for work, whilst Scotty and I set to work vandalising the garden. The trees at the bottom of the garden were indeed apple trees and were covered with tiny apples. The neighbour across the road told us they were Bramleys, ideal for cooking, the same as the factory processed. Cultivating this garden was not going to be easy. I concentrated on the area between the path and the neighbour's driveway.

Frozen In Time

The vast area on the other side would have to wait. I was afraid that if I wandered into it I might never return.

At work Karl was still doing his time and motion bit. Plans were afoot for a radical change in the ways peas were frozen, packed on trays and frozen in a tunnel for two hours was an awful waste of time. There had to be a better way.

When 8pm. arrived I thought about Steve and Melanie. Would they sort something out? I did hope so. Steve was popular with all the women but eventually one has to choose, unless one wants to be a playboy all one's life. When things were quiet on the factory floor, by that I mean when I wasn't in demand, there was a certain retreat in the boiler house where Bert reigned supreme. Between the two great boilers, he had a comfortable chair from which he could see all his gauges and keep control of the need for steam. He was like an engine driver snug in his warm cab. One could always go there for a warm up. At 11pm Steve arrived. I didn't even give him time to put his wellys on.

"Well" I said "did you see her?"

"Yes. She was there."

"Good-and?"

"Well when she saw me arrive she nearly walked out but Josie talked her into staying and then she left us alone. I explained why I was with Christine."

"And did she believe you?"

"She was sceptical at first, But when I offered to take her to the house where Christine bought the gear she relented."

"So?"

"I think I'm on probation."

"Thank heavens for that" I said relieved.

"You know John" he added "I really like Melanie. I didn't realise how much till yesterday and today when I realised we might have been finished...."

"Oh dear" I mocked "How are the mighty fallen?"

"Yes" he said quietly "It's scary isn't it."

Chapter 21

July came, and soon it would be time for me and Steve to change shifts. I wasn't looking forward to it although it would mean Josie and I would have the evenings together once again. And then one morning Josie wasn't feeling well. She went right off her breakfast. I told her to have the day off. After all she'd been working hard putting in a full days work and then coming home to housework, washing and cleaning, all those things her mother had done for her previously. It was bound to take it's toll. I did my bit. I was quite good at cooking but we hardly had meals together. Anyway she insisted that she was all right and left for work as usual. When I saw her just after three she said she felt better which was good news. But the next morning the same thing happened again. She felt very sick. I was worried now and said she should see a doctor but she said she knew what it was. I asked her "It's nothing serious is it?"

She replied "It's serious all right" and when she saw the worried look on my face she smiled and said "I think I'm pregnant." It took just a few seconds to take this in then I said "Pregnant! Are you sure?"

"Pretty sure."

"Oh My darling" I held her tightly, "that's wonderful." Then I released her. "Well you're not going to work then."

"Of course I am."

"But you can't if you're not well."

"It's just morning sickness. It's not an illness."

"But that's what Melanie had, and she stopped working"

"Yes, but I'm not Melanie." Then I said all the things that pregnant fathers say, about resting, not lifting heavy things, and surely cycling must be bad. When I had finished, the only concession that Josie would make was to visit the doctor to confirm her suspicions.

"Well, I'll take you to work on the scooter."

"But how am I going to get home. You'll be working."
"Oh yes. I'd forgotten."
"Look. I promise I'll eat something later. It's just early morning I feel sick." So I had to content myself with that compromise. "Oh and this is our secret. Ok?"
"Okay" I agreed "But I'll make an appointment with the doctor." To which she agreed. My thoughts were all in a turmoil for the rest of the day. I rode up to the phone box and made an appointment for the next day at 1pm. with her doctor in North Walsham. This way I could take her and bring her back before my shift at 3pm. I went up to the top bedroom and looked around with a view to it being a nursery. At the moment all it had in it was a single bed which someone had given us. There was nothing on the floor. I broke the news to Scotty as I couldn't tell anyone else and she seemed pleased. She could now climb stairs without any difficulty and was very boisterous. At 3pm. I was back at work. I wanted to tell everyone but of course I couldn't and I hoped my face didn't give it away. I found Josie as soon as possible and I thought she looked pale but she assured me she was okay. I told her about the appointment and she was a little surprised that I'd acted so promptly but agreed it was all right.

The next day I picked her up from work at lunchtime. I hadn't wanted her to go to work at all but she insisted. We went home for a quick sandwich and then set off for the doctor's. It wasn't a long delay before she was seen and I waited impatiently for her to come out. When she did she insisted on us leaving the surgery before confirming that she was indeed pregnant and the baby was due in March. We were both overjoyed. We had had every intention of starting a family whenever it happened, whether sooner or later. It just happened to be sooner. We had no thought as to the cost or the loss of income. It was what we wanted and we couldn't have been happier. We decided that her mum should be the first to know so we made a detour to Upper Street to break the news. Fiona was of course surprised to see us both in the middle of the day and was even more surprised at the news. Of course she was delighted for us but had hoped that we would have waited longer until we had a bit of money behind us. But what was done was done and she promised to help wherever she could. I was naturally now keen to share our good news and Josie conceded that now that Fiona knew, Melanie would know and then everyone would, so it was alright to tell. Anyway, having time off work would be bound to lead to speculation so rather than lie it would be easier to tell the truth. This I did when I eventually started work and Tosh was delighted with the news as were May and Phyllis and I knew it would soon be common knowledge.

Middle of July, time for change of shifts between Steve and myself.
    It wasn't so bad for me at the change over because I went home at midnight and didn't return till 11pm. the next day. Steve on the other hand went home at 8am. and was due to return after a sleep at 3pm.,7 hours later, so to ease his first day Tosh gave him till 5pm. so he could have longer to sleep if necessary. I now had all day and evening at home which meant I could keep an eye on Josie throughout the evening.
    My first shot at nights wasn't as bad as I'd anticipated. There was enough going on to keep me occupied so I wasn't tired but the hardest thing to get used to was the change in eating habits. My stomach wasn't keen to change. Tasting peas at three or four in the morning made my stomach rebel and as for eating a lunch after midnight it positively refused to cooperate, so much so that I had to make a visit to the nurse who gave me a concoction to drink which seemed to have ginger in it and it worked. Gradually my stomach changed shifts with me. The good thing about this shift was knowing that Josie was safely in bed with Scotty to guard her, for although she was still growing she made a lot of noise if anybody approached the house.
    The women on night shift were different to those on day shift. They were a much more rowdy crowd and no doubt some were there for more than work. With all those students on the

site it was inevitable that some matchmaking went on. There were rumours that the lunch break around 1am. was used for more than eating. One woman, for she wasn't a girl, called Kathy was at the forefront in the hunting game, and those who were compliable knew where to go. This was not acceptable to the management of course, though little could be said about what people did in their own time. Kieran, our student, often applied for extra shifts after the day shift as did many other students for there was always work that needed doing. He was seen with Kathy more than once.

One characteristic of being pregnant is the craving for certain foods. Josie loved canned fruit and I had the means of getting it for her. As I said before, during a canning run it was necessary to take finished cans from the line and open, and taste the contents. The rest was thrown away. Not now it wasn't. Tosh had shown us that a kilner jar with a tight lid was ideal for taking such waste home where it would be appreciated. I made the most of this whenever fruit was the subject of canning. Josie loved it, especially plums and plum juice. But she appreciated just as much strawberries, gooseberries or raspberries.

One thing I remember in particular about the early mornings, even in July was the cold. Around 5 or 6am.the temperature dropped and I often found myself in the boiler house, the one hot place, for a bit of warmth. In the boiler house at night I was aware of the sound of crickets. Apparently they make a noise with their back legs, a sort of click, for what reason I'm not sure, but the repetitiveness of the noise depends on the heat. Someone said that if you counted the number of clicks in a minute you could work out the temperature of the room. I think there was something else to this formula but I never proved it right or wrong. But one of my most remaining pleasures was standing at the door of the boiler house and seeing the dawn rise. Only then did you appreciate the mists on the fields and marvel at the wonder of yet a new day. Perhaps its association with the fact that I would soon be going home had something to do with it.

The change over of shifts was a blessing in disguise for Fiona, for Steve and Melanie seemed to be on course again and now that Steve was doing evening shifts, Melanie hardly went out and took her responsibility with Cindy much more seriously. This relieved Fiona and she in turn was able to visit Josie occasionally in the evening and so do her bit for both of her girls in some way. And strangely enough Christine never was with Josie in her pregnancy as she had been with Melanie. We had thought that she might be. In fact she made sure that she didn't do any jobs that might involve heavy lifting, and took a motherly interest in her. Far from the jealousy of Melanie she took on a surrogacy role for Josie. All this was very pleasing for me and took away some of the worries that I as an expectant father had. The one worry that couldn't be dismissed was that I couldn't be there for her in the morning when she was at her worst. My shift finished at 8am. which was the time hers started. So I insisted that we saw each other at this time each day to make sure she was all right. That way if she didn't turn up I'd know to hurry home. It wasn't ideal at all but it was the best we could do.

The fraternisations carried on during the nightshifts, and as long as it didn't interfere with working hours a blind eye was turned. It was obvious talking to Kieran that he had made a few conquests, and not all were single girls either. I didn't mention any of this to Josie. I didn't want her worrying that I might be tempted too. She had nothing to fear though. I was perfectly happy with her and wanted no other. But matters came to a head one night after lunch break when one of the junior foremen couldn't be found and Kathy hadn't returned to her place on the line. Suspicions were roused when no response came from him after a call over the tannoy system. The senior foreman decided to make his own search. He took a torch and searched around the outside of the factory. He finally came across his prey when behind the cooling towers his torch revealed a bare male bottom en flagrante delicto. Needless to say the manager Rupert Beard gave him his cards the next day and Kathy never returned.

Sleeping during the day was difficult at first. I wasn't used to sleeping with the daylight coming through the curtains. It was a bit better when I hung a spare blanket over the window then it seemed more like night. I got used to it after a couple of weeks but then I was disturbed one morning when I heard someone coming in the house and Scotty began to bark. Putting on my dressing gown I crept downstairs to seek out the intruder. I opened the door to the living room and there on the chaise longue sat Josie obviously upset. I crossed to her "Whatever's the matter love?" I asked.

"They brought me home" she said crying "I was sick at work. I feel awful."

"Oh my dear" I said sitting beside her and trying to comfort her "It's all been too much for you."

"It's the smell" she cried "I couldn't stand the smell. It made me feel so ill."

"Then you won't have to smell it again. You can stay at home."

"But we need the money."

"No we don't. Not that much. We can manage. There's no way you're going back to be made ill anymore. You and the baby are too important to me to risk that. We may never be wealthy but at least we'll be happy. Now, how about a nice cup of tea?"

"Oh no!" she said and rushed to the bathroom.

That was the last time she worked at the factory. She still felt sick in the mornings but at least she could cope with it at home and I was there to help her. It meant I could relax a bit knowing she wasn't suffering unnecessarily. So Josie took charge of the house proper and was able to take Scotty for walks. That in itself wasn't easy for it was a very busy road and she was an excitable dog and there were no pathways. She would walk her up to the Arch to the post office which was situated in one of the quaint houses set each side of it. They were square, two storey houses made of brick and flint and all the windows matched those in the Arch except of course they had glass in them whilst those in the Arch didn't. Or else she would walk upto Scottow which was our nearest shop to purchase a few things or just for the walk. Very occasionally she would catch the bus to Norwich to see my mum for the day. This was quite difficult for her because even bus travel made her feel queasy. When she wasn't doing these things she would potter about in the garden. There were always things to do there. All the vegetables I had sown were doing very well but having cultivated the soil a new menace in the shape of moles appeared. I was watering a row of beans with a hose pipe and just laid the hose at the base of the row whilst I did something else. Some time later I returned expecting the area to be well flooded. To my surprise it was bone dry and yet the hose was still running. Closer inspection revealed that the water was disappearing down a hole. It had found a mole run and totally flooded it. I knew that was what it was because I had seen mole hills in the garden and as I walked that area the whole run collapsed with the action of the water, revealing the extent of the run. I hoped that at least I might have discouraged the moles from coming there but to my annoyance the next day I saw the whole run had been pushed back up again by the little devils and several of my plants were out of the ground. This called for desperate measures so I borrowed a mole trap from Tosh with full instructions and inserted it into the run. I won't go into details for the squeamish but that week I caught six and my problem was solved and my plants saved. For those of you who are about to stop reading in sympathy with the moles I should point out that they had entered my garden under the neighbour's drive from the field on the other side and until I started cultivating my soil they were quite content to stay there in acres of worm rich soil. They were the trespassers not I. I felt I was defending my territory like a real countryman and relished the feeling.

Our next intruder was very different. Coming home from work just after 8am. I unlocked the door and greeted Scotty who we always kept downstairs at night. Josie was still in bed so I went upstairs to see her. As I passed the small living room I just instinctively opened the door which was dark as the curtains were drawn. There was a flurry of noise which so shocked me that I shut the door quickly. Whatever was it? Something was in there, that was certain. Just then Josie appeared, woken by the various noises of dog barking and door slamming.

"What is it?" she asked "What's the matter?"

"There's something in there" I whispered.

"How can there be?" she queried. "I was in there last night and I closed the door when I went to bed."

"I tell you there's something in there. Look I'll show you." and once again I tentatively opened the door. There was a flurry of noise and I shut the door again quickly. "There. I told you."

"Whatever is it?" Josie said, now as concerned as I was.

"I don't know" I said "but I'm going to find out. I'm going to put the light on. I can't see a thing in there" Cautiously I opened the door just far enough to get my hand in and switched on the light. Everything was quiet. I pushed the door open a bit more and there sitting on the back of one of the chairs was an owl staring right back at me. "It's an owl" I said.

"Oh let me see" said Josie and together we stood and looked at this creature with it's big eyes looking straight back at us. "Isn't it lovely" said Josie. "Lovely it might be" I said "but how the hell do we get it out of there and how did it get there in the first place?"

"Down the chimney" Josie said. Then I remembered that for two or three days we had found bits of brick and mortar in the fireplace and had suspected that the chimney might be crumbling.

"It must have been in there for days" I surmised "and it couldn't get out."

"Till now" added Josie. "So how do we get rid of it?"

"Well I'm certainly not going in there and trying to pick it up" I'd heard about owls landing on people's heads and clawing at their eyes and I didn't want it happening to me.

"Can't we open the window?"

"It's possible I suppose."

"I'll do it."

"No! I'll do it. You watch the bird." So once again I opened the door. It still sat there. I pushed the door right open and cautiously edged round the door to the window. I drew the curtains with one eye on it, then I opened the window. It didn't move. I crept back to the door and stepped out of the room. Relieved, I closed the door. "Well it's up to it now." Josie watched through the front door window whilst I went outside. It wasn't long before it appeared and immediately flew towards the barns mobbed by several smaller birds. Thankful I returned indoors and we surveyed the room. There were numerous scratch marks on the ceiling but apart from that there was no other damage. Our only hope was that it wouldn't return and thankfully it never did.

Chapter 22

The next two months passed by quite uneventful. Needless to say I thoroughly enjoyed having Josie at home all day. I slept during the morning and part of the afternoon but we were then together till she went to bed and I went to work. Then in September I was back on day shift once again, and the factory was slowing down. I even had weekends off and this meant that when there was an Autumn Show just through the Arch and on the Estate we were able to attend together. We took Scotty with us. She was now fully grown and too much for Josie to handle in her state so I held the lead along the road and in the show. Josie's dad had entered some vegetables for it was a show for exhibitors to display their best produce in the hope of winning a trophy. Josie was visibly pregnant by now and it wasn't far from home so we didn't have far to walk. It was a fine afternoon and there were marquees for all the exhibits. We strolled through them all, admiring the best of the area in every class until we came to the vegetables. There were some very good ones, particularly in the carrot, leek and parsnip categories but when we came to the cabbages there were only three entries. There was a 'First', a 'Second' and a 'Not up to show Standard'. I called Josie's attention to them and we both looked at each other and laughed, for back in our garden we had a row of enormous cabbages, every one better than the best in show. If only we'd known, but it never occurred to us to enter. After all we were just novice gardeners. It certainly showed just how good our soil was.

We met Peter and Fiona and he showed us some of his entries. He had a 'First' for leeks, a 'Second' for carrots, and a 'Highly Commended for potatoes. We congratulated and commiserated. I asked if he'd entered a cabbage but he hadn't. I was glad.

After the Show they came back to ours for a cup of tea and

Peter looked around the garden. He was impressed by what we'd achieved so far. When he came to the cabbages he looked then said "Not bad" and walked on. I asked Fiona about Steve and Melanie and she said that things seemed quite good. She was particularly pleased that Steve seemed to adore Cindy and though this was a good thing she feared that Melanie was a little jealous and this had led to one or two rows. "I don't know how he puts up with her sometimes" she said. I resolved then never to let Josie be number two in my life when the baby was born.

It was in October that I lost Josie. It was a routine visit to my parents. She had gone for the day as she did occasionally. I knew the time the bus would drop her at our house and as it was dark I was going to wait for her by the road. It was not a designated bus stop. In those days the driver would drop you wherever you asked him to. Unfortunately there was no street lighting and you had to keep an eye on where you were. Josie had difficulty seeing in the dark and had finally had to wear glasses. On top of that it was raining heavily. I noticed that the bus was early. I didn't have time to get outside but to my amazement and worry the bus didn't stop. I got to the road and looked after it but as far as I could tell it never stopped at all till it was out of sight. "*Oh god!*" I thought, "*don't tell me she's got off at the wrong place*". I had all sorts of worries about her stranded somewhere along the road in this weather. I looked back along the road but it was pointless trying to see anything so I hurriedly got my scooter out and put on my waterproofs and drove back up the road. I looked on both sides of the road, imagining her struggling along. "*What if she's fallen into a ditch or something.*" I thought. I was increasingly worried. I got all the way to Scottow Three Horse Shoes pub. That was lit up. She wouldn't have got off before this so she must have got off after our house. I turned round and made my way home. Maybe she was home. I stopped and called in. No she wasn't there. There was nothing for it but to search the other way. I rode slowly upto and through the Arch. Nobody was walking along the road at all. I blamed myself for not being at the roadside with my torch when the bus went by. She would have seen it and got up from her seat to be let off. But then it occurred to me that she might have missed the bus and still be in Norwich. I decided to ring my brother Philip. He was the only one on the phone and in the past he had taken Josie from my parents to the bus station. I made my way to the phone box and dialled his number. He answered and confirmed that he had given Josie a lift to the station in time to catch the bus. Now I was really worried. My last hope that she had missed the bus had gone. I was convinced that she was out here somewhere, lost, pregnant, and soaking wet. I rang the police. They told me to wait at our house and someone would come. I went back and waited. About 15 minutes later a police car arrived with two officers inside. I explained the situation and they said they would go along the road and look for her. By now I was thoroughly drenched but I wasn't going to go inside. I wanted to be there when she arrived. Shortly after the police returned. They hadn't found her. They then began to ask me questions. Basically they were asking if I was telling them the truth. 'Had we had a row?' 'Was this nothing more than a family squabble?' I got really angry and frustrated with them and they were calming me down just as a car drove up behind theirs. It was my brother's car and Josie got out of it. She didn't seem at all perturbed and wondered why the police car was there. I explained, and asked her what had happened. Apparently the Autumn bus timetable had come into force and the bus had left earlier. The only thing she could think to do was contact Phillip so she had gone back to my parents who rang up Phillip who kindly brought her home. She was very sorry for the trouble she had caused but there was no way she could let me know. The police officers were very understanding and I could see them grinning to themselves as they wished us goodnight and drove away. We thanked Phillip too and he left. "I'm really sorry John" she said "but there was nothing I could do."

    I was a mixture of relief, frustration, and anger, plus I was totally drenched and the only thing I could think to do was get indoors and have a hot bath which I did. We had come dangerously close to our first row and yet it was nobody's fault. During the bath I was able to be grateful that it could have been a lot worse. All the things I thought might have happened to her hadn't and I contented myself with that.

Although we had made good headway with the garden immediately in front of the house there remained a vast area to the right of the property which we hadn't been able to cultivate. Since May it had been covered in ground elder and blackthorn and was a major task. Speaking to someone about it they suggested that geese were great ground clearers. Plus you have the bonus of geese eggs and if you have a gander and a goose you could even breed from them. I put this thought to Josie and she saw no problems with that idea so I investigated it further. All that was needed was a pen of three foot chicken wire around the land you wanted them in, and a gate preferably, and that was it. Of course a pond would have been better but that we didn't have so we'd do without. I made enquiries about purchasing a gander and two geese and found someone who would sell and deliver so I went ahead with the deal. First though I had to build the pen. It cost a little for the materials but I put it up very quickly. Apparently geese don't have a wander lust. They are content to stay in their appointed place so I didn't need to peg down every piece of netting. In fact I was told that after a while of making a designated area for them you could remove the netting and they still wouldn't stray beyond the area they had got used to. Time would tell if this was true or not.

The day arrived for delivery of our feathered friends and a car arrived. I had expected a van but the driver opened the boot and there they were. The journey hadn't pleased them and there was quite a bit of nervous goose droppings in the boot but he had been prepared for that with a piece of polythene covering the floor. They began their noise as soon as they saw daylight. I hadn't a clue how to handle them but he showed me that as soon as you had a hold on their necks you could put your arm round them and lift them up. Sounded easy but they weren't willing participants in having their necks held. He just distracted them with one hand whilst grabbing their necks with the other. I let him remove all three and place them in their des. res. They then set off to explore, honking as they went. I paid the man and he wished me luck and left. Once again I felt like a true countryman as Josie and I admired our new residents. They had a big bowl of water and we threw scraps of food in to them but they were out of sight exploring the other side of the pen and we left them to it.

Whilst we saw some possible future income from the geese an unexpected present income came to us from our two Bramley apple trees. They were laden with huge cooking apples. Some we picked for ourselves and laid on the shelves in the cellar for future use but that still left a lot on the trees. Now was the time when we were processing apples in the factory so I enquired at the field office if they wanted any more. They agreed to buy what we had and the next day several bushel boxes appeared at the bottom of the garden for us to fill. This was a job we could do together so we started by picking those we could reach. Then I climbed up the trees with a basket and handed them down to Josie. As usual with fruit the best were at the very top and I didn't want to be thwarted by them so I tried many precarious manoeuvres to procure them against Josie's warnings that the branches might not be strong enough. In the end, with nothing more than a few scratches, we filled three boxes. The next day, just as they had arrived, the boxes disappeared and a week later we received a cheque for them. It wasn't a lot but it felt good. What a shame we didn't have more trees.

Now it was getting colder we were beginning to light fires for the house felt the chill. Initially we lit the fire in the downstairs living room because it heated the water by the back boiler. There was a brick shed on our side of the barns which I supposed was once the outside toilet. We now used it as a coal shed. Whenever we could however we burnt wood, but only if we found it lying around the garden or the barns, we couldn't afford to buy that as well as coal. I had noticed that on the factory site there was a pile of discarded wood that had no particular use and I must have expressed my wish to Tosh that I could carry it home, which of course was impossible. To my surprise however on arriving home the next day I saw this pile of wood just beside the path. When I asked Josie if she knew anything about it she said Tosh had turned up in a truck and left it there. She supposed I knew all about it, which of course I didn't. But I made a point of thanking him sincerely the next day. He just grinned and said "No problem." That was the nature of the man.

That at least is how I saw him, a kind, considerate man, a man who could do any job in the factory and without whom the factory would be the poorer. Yet he wasn't always appreciated. From the work floor to the management he was taken for granted. Some sniggered behind his back as people do when they lack the skill of those they mock. Others like Rupert Beard treated him with less than respect when on the few occasions he deigned to visit us at the lab. In fact, since my interview with him 19 months previously he had never spoken a word to me. But I owed Tosh a lot and had great respect for him, as I believe Steve did also.

One cannot be in the country without having contact with animals and we had already started to integrate with them. However, animals have their rightful place and humans theirs, and sometimes they are better apart as one event showed us and could have been tragic. I was not involved in this incident being at work but Josie had planned to visit her mum and as this was difficult without transport, the local vicar, a friend of Fiona's had offered to pick her up and take her there. All went well. He arrived and they set off. They were nearly there when the car came to a halt and closer inspection showed it had run out of petrol. He was very apologetic but fortunately they weren't far from their destination. They could have walked along the road but he suggested a cut across the field would be quicker. Josie wasn't so sure, especially as the field in question contained some bullocks. They were however well away from the part they needed to cross. So in the end Josie agreed. They climbed over the gate and set off. They hadn't gone far when the bullocks spied them and together set off towards them. It became obvious that unless they both got a move on the bullocks would reach them.

"Come on! Run!" he shouted and set off for the fence. Josie needed no persuasion and set off after him. It was a close thing as they only just got there before the herd and unceremoniously clambered over the wooden fence. "Wow! That was close" he said "Are you all right?"

"I think so" answered Josie out of breath.

"I don't suppose they would have hurt us" he offered in mitigation "They were probably just curious." They continued the rest of the journey without incident but when they told Fiona what had happened she was furious with him. "Didn't you know she was five months pregnant. You could have caused her to have a miscarriage." He was devastated and so apologetic but to be fair to him, nobody had told him. He insisted she sat down and had a drink and refused to leave until he was absolutely sure she had suffered no ill effects from their escapade. When it appeared she was all right, although one never knows about after shocks, and Fiona had calmed down she said to him on a lighter note "If this child grows up afraid of cows I shall blame it on you." No doubt he said a prayer for Josie when he left but I was certainly not impressed when I heard what happened. "He must have been a blind vicar not to notice you're pregnant" I said angrily but then she did have a big coat on so once again there was some excuse.

I kept in touch with what was going on in the Fisher household through Josie but also through Steve who had confided in me that he and Melanie were having a stormy relationship. I hoped they would sort it out for their and Cindy Louise's sake for Steve was very fond of her, and now she was seven months old and very cute he could see himself being a father to her, so it came as quite a shock to me when he told me it was all over.

He was tired of Melanie's jealousy and couldn't take it any more though the break with Cindy was just as painful as the break with Melanie. Fiona had tried talking to her as had her father, both who thought Steve was a good match for her but she had just said things like "He isn't any fun any more" or "All he thinks of is staying in with Cindy" and when they pointed out that he was about 8 years older than her and probably wanted to settle down, she just said that she didn't. When I told Josie, she too was very upset for we had pinned our hopes on every thing working out.

"Well there's not much we can do about it." I said. But Josie just said "I suppose not."

Now that we had geese as well as a dog we had double warning of anyone approaching the house. Scotty was of the breed of dog bred to round up sheep and she delighted in running round the geese pen and acting out her inbred role. She never actually went in with the geese although she could now jump the fence if she so wished. I think she had a sort of respect for those long snake like necks and she preferred to be brave out side the pen. But her ability to jump the fence was causing other problems. She was a very sociable animal and loved people and when ever she heard any body, even if they were walking along the road she had to go and say hello. This caused a lot of distress to Josie because she had to go and retrieve her and apologise to the people she was harassing, even though she meant them no harm. And as she grew bigger it became more of a problem.

We were discovering just how cold our house was as we entered Winter proper. Sometimes we would have a roaring fire and we could hear the water boiling in the tank in the airing cupboard and yet we felt cold. Part of the reason was having three doors leading into the room, each from cold areas and they didn't fit terribly well. Plus there was no central heating or double glazing so the blast of air from fields all around came straight in to the house. This was when we decided that for the evenings we would light a fire in the smaller lounge, have the television in there and with the one door, shut out the world. And it worked, though we had to let the other fire out because we couldn't afford two. So during the day we heated our water, and to a degree the downstairs, and in the evenings we heated ourselves. Little did we know then that this was going to be one of the coldest winters we would ever experience.

Chapter 23

We were looking forward to our first Christmas in our own house and anticipated sharing it with our families. We would of course need more chairs for we were seriously short of them but we hoped to address this problem in time. However events took over of such a serious matter that all thoughts of celebration went out of our minds. It concerned Cindy Louise. Fiona was still looking after her during the day whilst Melanie was working at the factory. It wasn't easy for Steve with her working there for he still felt deeply for her but he avoided her when he could. Nobody in the factory could understand her attitude towards him but several of the other girls were glad he was free and fancied their chances with him. However, it was on a cold but sunny day that Fiona had pushed the baby out in her pram as she often did for the exercise. She stopped at a friend's house, only intending to stop for little while. Cindy was well wrapped up and the sun was on the pram so she left her asleep outside. When she returned after about 5 minutes she got the shock of her life. The pram was still there but Cindy wasn't. She looked all around the pram thinking she had fallen out but she wasn't anywhere. She wanted to scream but she couldn't. Just then her friend followed her out. She saw the look on Fiona's face and then a glance at the pram told her what was wrong. "Oh my god!" she gasped "Where's Cindy?"
"She's gone!" shrieked Fiona, regaining her voice. "Somebody's taken her!"
"But they can't have. It's not possible."
"But she's not here. Is she? I left her here. She was asleep. Somebody's taken her I tell you. Oh please tell me it's not true. Please! Oh my god! Where is she? Where is she ?" and she broke down crying hysterically. This brought the next door neighbour out as well to ask whatever was the matter. The word spread quickly. Nobody had seen anything. Most people

were indoors on such a cold day. A search began immediately along the High Street and lanes. Fiona was in a terrible state. She wanted to help but was in no state to. Her friend took her in and made her a cup of tea but it could not assuage the feeling of guilt and despair. "What am I going to tell her mum? What am I going to tell Melanie? It's all my fault. I shouldn't have left her there. It was only for 5minutes." As many people as could joined in the search but to no avail. Finally it was decided to call the police.

The first we knew about it was when a police car arrived at the factory and a constable asked to see Melanie. We had a good view of the offices from the lab and when we saw Melanie talking to the police both Steve and I were out there like a flash. The reality of what had happened had just hit Melanie as we got there. "Oh Steve" she cried "someone's stolen Cindy" and she burst into tears. "Oh my god!" gasped Steve and he put his arm round her to comfort her.

"We don't quite know what's happened yet" said the policeman "It appears the child has gone missing from her pram."

"When was this?" asked Steve still holding the sobbing Melanie.

"About two hours ago. We've got people out looking for her. If you'd like to come with us miss we'll drive you there."

"I'll come too" said Steve. "I'll come in my car it might be useful. Try not to worry Melanie I'm sure we'll find her safe and well." and he shot off back to the lab to discard his coat and hat and get his car whilst the tearful Melanie went in the police car accompanied by a woman police constable. "You get off" I told him "I'll explain to Tosh" and he disappeared. There seemed no point in going with him though I would have liked to but we couldn't both desert our posts and he was the obvious choice. He was more involved than me and would be more comfort to Melanie. I felt there was nothing to be gained by informing Josie at this stage and hoped all would be resolved before long but I couldn't settle at work and was desperate for some news. '*Who on earth could do such a thing?*'

When Melanie arrived home and found out what had happened, she naturally berated her mother for what had happened. "How could you?" she yelled. "How could you do such a thing?"

"I am so sorry" cried Fiona "How was I to know that this would happen? Oh I'm so sorry." and she convulsed in tears, comforted by Peter who had been brought home from work.

"I'm going to look for her" said Melanie defiantly and left the room.

"I'll come with you" said Steve.

"The police have organised a proper search." said Peter calling after her.

"Let her go" said a police sergeant "She needs to feel she's doing something."

Indeed a proper search was conducted, calling on every house in the Frankfort and Upper Street areas of Sloley. Barns and out houses were searched, but as daylight disappeared they were no further forward. The police were convinced that she was still nearby and asked for the addresses of any local relations. This of course included Josie and Fiona begged them not to bother her but they said that they had to cover every angle. Which angle they had in mind they wouldn't say. Having heard nothing by the end of my shift I went home to break the news to Josie. I knew she would want to go over there and I was prepared for that. What I wasn't prepared for was a police car outside our house. I hurried in and found a police officer in conversation with her. It was clear he had already told her what had happened. "Oh John this is terrible" she said nearly in tears "Poor little Cindy."

"I know" I said hugging her "It's the worst kind of news but I'm sure they'll find her soon."

"Would you mind if we had a look around sir?" asked the policeman.

"What here?" I gasped.

"Yes sir. Just to eliminate you from our enquiries"

"Eliminate!" Josie said incredulously "Surely you don't think we had anything to do with it. She's my niece. I love her. We wouldn't do anything to harm her."

The policeman kept his composure. "Just to make sure miss" and he set off across the living room towards the stairs.

"Let him go" I said to Josie. I knew the effrontery of it had added to her upset. "He's just doing his job" He came back quite soon, obviously satisfied.

"Have you looked in the cellar? Perhaps she's under the apples." asked Josie sarcastically determined to get the last word in.

"That will be all sir, madam. I'm sorry this is so upsetting but it could hardly be otherwise could it under the cicumstances. I'm sure we'll find her safe and well. We usually do. Goodnight sir, madam." and he left.

"I want to go to mum's" said Josie putting on her coat and helmet and I didn't argue because I wanted to as well. We needed to know what was going on. Was there any progress?

The house was the saddest I'd ever seen it. Fiona looking much older with the worry. Peter pacing up and down, Melanie still whimpering and a policewoman still trying to glean that little bit of information which might make the breakthrough. Josie went straight to Melanie and the two sisters wept in unison. "Where's Steve?" I asked Peter.

"He's still out looking" he said "but what can you see in the dark?" I decided to go out too. It was better than staying and issuing words that meant nothing at such times as this. There were a few more lights about than one usually sees in the country at night and I concluded that Steve wasn't the only person out looking. One police car was still outside the house but otherwise the police presence was minimal. I found Steve returning to the house. He was thoroughly dejected. He wanted to carry on but he realised the futility of it. We went back in the house. Melanie looked up hopefully every time someone came into the room but the answer was always the same "Nothing I'm afraid. Sorry."

Finally the police left saying they'd be back first thing.

Steve asked if he could stay on the settee because he too wanted to be there first thing. Of course they agreed and he went to the phone box to ring home so they wouldn't worry about him. I decided we could do no more and reluctantly took a very distressed Josie home. I knew none of us were going to get much sleep that night.

The next day came and the police arrived early. Everyone was up, had been for some time, not having slept much if at all. Apparently the police had called on every house and spoken to the occupiers. Where no one was at home they would call again today. They were thinking of widening their search though and were using all means at their disposal to find Cindy. This brought little comfort to anyone and Steve vowed to keep looking locally. I took Josie over there to be what help she could. There was no way she would have stayed at home, then I returned to work. Tosh and the managers quite understood Steve's absence and wished them all luck in their search.

Steve decided to investigate for himself. Not every house had been searched in the village. The only ones that had, had been relatives in the area and he asked to see the list. There were only three names on it in the area, including ours. One name wasn't on it and he decided to keep his hunch to himself, for that was all it was, and he set out to follow it. He knew where to go because Melanie had pointed it out to him once on their walks around the village with Cindy. It was a run down farm property which had seen better days and Steve went up to it and surveyed it, cautiously because he knew there were dogs there. The police would have called round and talked to the occupier so he saw no point in repeating the exercise. Instead he decided to look round the back. No dogs barked.

The back was as unkempt as the front and he crept upto the window and looked in. He hoped he wouldn't be seen for he had no valid reason for being there, only suspicion. His eyes adjusted to the light and he scanned the room, and there sitting in a chair was Tom's mother holding a baby. His heart leapt. His hunch was right. It had to be Cindy. Tom was her only son and her husband had left them both years ago. How was he to get her out safely? And where were the dogs? He decided to follow the house round and as he turned the corner he found them. They were both chained up and when they saw him they began to bark and strain at their chains. Immediately Steve retraced his steps. He knew that she must now be curious about the noise and he crept back to the window. He was just in time to see her put Cindy down and go to the front door. After a few seconds he heard her rebuking the dogs and knew she was out of the house. Quick as a flash he tried the back door and found it open. It opened into the kitchen and a door to the right he knew led into the living room where he had seen Cindy. He knew there was no time to lose and entering he saw Cindy lying on a blanket on the floor. As fast as he could he gathered her up in his arms and headed for the back door. He was just going out as he heard the front door close. Not stopping to close the door behind him he ran as fast as he could down the drive till he came to the road and nearly ran into the arms of a policeman who was revisiting a house that was on their list from yesterday. The policeman thought it was his lucky day and was about to arrest him on suspicion of kidnapping when a very distraught woman, Tom's mother, came screaming down the drive claming this man had stolen her granddaughter. The policeman was confused and called for backup. He was almost accusing Steve of serial kidnapping. Steve tried to explain and finally with a policewoman there to deal with Tom's mum Steve was escorted back to home with Cindy to prove his story. What a reception he got as he appeared with her and placed her in the arms of her mother. There were more tears and kissing and thanking and still more tears of joy as they all crowded around. The policeman said that a doctor would need to check her over but she certainly seemed none the worse for her day away. And when Steve told them where he'd found her they were livid, and Melanie swore she'd never let her see her again.

 The police arrived shortly after having searched the farmhouse and found signs of the baby having been there. Tom's mother had been arrested but the sergeant said she kept mumbling about her grandchild being stolen. She was clearly not in her right mind. He said that had they known that she was the child's grandmother they would have searched her house yesterday.

"Funny thing families" said the sergeant as he wished us well and left.

"Well I'd better get back to work too" said Steve. "John and the others will be waiting for news." Fiona came to him and hugged him and Peter shook his hand "How can we ever thank you ?" they said.

"There's no need." he replied "She means a great deal to me" and he left. He was just opening his car when Melanie came hurrying up.

"Steve! Please don't go" she called.

"I must do some work."

"What you did today was fantastic"

"I only did what any....."

"....father would do? I know she means a lot to you."

"I'm pretty fond of her mother too."

"I know. Steve, I've been such a silly, selfish, childish fool. I've grown up these last 24 hours. Come back after work."

"Melanie, if this is out of gratitude, I'd rather you didn't."

"Oh we're grateful of course, Cindy and I, but what I realise now is that we both need you. I need you. I want you. Please say you'll come back." She placed her hands on his chest. For a moment they just looked at each other, then taking her hands in his he said "Take good care of my two girls. I'll see you after work" and with a smile they said goodbye and he drove off.

The news spread through the factory like wild fire and everyone was delighted for all the family. Of course we didn't know the full extent of the part Steve had played till the following day, but it was clear from his demeanour that something had happened to Steve, reminiscent of what happened to me the day Josie agreed to be my wife.

Cindy was given the all clear from the doctor. Tom's mother was treated leniently because of her mental state, and Melanie

Frozen In Time

blamed herself for not keeping her promise to keep her acquainted with Cindy. Steve and Melanie began a much stronger relationship, which we all hoped would continue.

Chapter 24

That Christmas was wonderful. As we had planned, the whole of Josie's family, including Steve, joined us for Christmas day and our usually spacious house suddenly seemed less spacious. We had fires in both rooms and a turkey cooking in the kitchen so the house felt warmer than usual. Because of the shortage of chairs on which to sit and eat we brought the table from the kitchen into the lounge and used the chaise longue down one side. This accommodated two of us so we were able to all sit around the table for lunch. It was a happy time and lovely to see Melanie and Steve interacting with Cindy like a real family. *'Next year'* I thought that will be us. Boxing day we spent at Fiona and Peter's but Melanie and Steve weren't there. They were at Steve's parents' house for the day. Another good sign we all thought. Later we went to my parents for a day and then all too soon the holiday period was over and we were back at work.

The winter of 63 was extremely cold. According to the Met.Office Records, the coldest since1740. Day after day the ground remained frozen solid and the nights were bitter. To warm our bedroom we had one of those round, Valor paraffin heaters but it had little effect on a big room. Then one morning we found we had no water. Everything was frozen. We tried heating the bathroom with the heater but with no success, so we consulted with our neighbours who had the same problem. He said he had been up into the loft and the tank was frozen so he had thawed it out and broken the ice. We had no access from our part of the house so we couldn't check it ourselves. Whatever he had done to the tank still hadn't helped us so he said he'd have another look. This time he went a bit further and discovered there was a second tank above our bathroom and he treated it the same. This time we got our water back. I think our water was from a bore well so there was no danger of that freezing but the tanks in the loft certainly did and from then on at night I kept the Valor heater in the bathroom. The cottages across the road weren't so lucky and resorted to collecting water from us till their supply was restored.

But so cold was it at night that we used two or three hot water bottles to heat the bed, but when we woke in the morning and put our hands on the eiderdown they came up wet. I concluded that our warm breath, the only source of heat above the bed, had condensed in the cold, forming this layer of moisture on the bed. It worried me that it could be dangerous for our health and particularly for Josie in her condition. This continuous cold was becoming a drain on our heating resources so I took to going over to the wood opposite, which ran along the road, and collecting sacks of fallen branches. They didn't have to be large bits, anything that burnt would do and this kept our fires burning throughout the day and eked out our limited supply of coal. After all I wasn't robbing anybody. I was tidying up the wood whilst keeping our house warm. I couldn't risk Josie getting cold and she was here all day whilst I was warm enough at the factory. It even occurred to me that I might be able to burn the cow dung which was bone dry in the sheds and which I had dug into the garden. After all I'd seen them do it in films somewhere in the Yukon in the depth of winter. But then I didn't know if it would give off any noxious fumes or smells which was the last thing Josie could cope with so I dismissed the idea.

Regretfully though the last thing Josie could cope with was Scotty. Both she and Josie had increased in size. She to a full grown lively dog and Josie to a very pregnant woman of 7 months, and she was too much for her to handle. Chiefly because in her excitement and friendliness she would keep jumping up her. Josie had long given up taking her for walks and we had no adequate means of keeping her in the garden and when I came home one day and found Josie in tears I knew that we had to make a decision.

"I just can't cope with her anymore" she sobbed, "She

almost knocks me over. I just can't cope." I hugged her and said I understood. I knew the only thing to do was get rid of her. As I said at the beginning I'm not really a dog person. My reason for getting one was for company for Josie and for her protection but we never anticipated this situation.

"Alright love we'll get rid of her" I said, but this just made her cry the more because she was genuinely fond of her. We both were. She was our first baby and we'd watched her grow up. "I'm sure there's some one out there who would love to have her and can give her a good home. What she needs is plenty of space to run and play and where she can be trained as a farm dog." This pacified her a bit. "You'll give her away then?" she said this more as if she didn't believe me rather than a plea. "No" I replied "We'll sell her."

"Sell her?"

"Yes. People give away things they don't value as a rule. We want her to go to a good home and that means she has to be valued and if someone values her enough they'll buy her." She saw the sense in this and agreed to let me advertise in the local shops. So I wrote three notes and placed them in shops in Worstead, Westwick and Scottow. The notes read 'For Sale- friendly, one year old, female, Border Collie. £3. Apply.....' and we waited for some response. As usual when decisions are made of this nature you begin to wonder if you've done the right thing and Josie, who was very weepy at the least little thing in her condition tried her hardest to compensate to her. She tried telling herself that things weren't really that bad, that it wasn't Scotty's fault, which we both knew anyway, and that perhaps we should keep her after all.

Then one day returning home, I found Josie tearful once again.

"A man called round today" she said "He wants to buy Scotty. He's got a farm at Swanton Morley and would love to have her for his children. He's coming back later. I told him when you'd be home" It sounded promising, especially that bit about children, for Scotty needed lots of love and affection, and had lots to give. True to his word the man returned and brought his son with him and as was his character, Scotty needed no introduction and treated everybody as a friend. She jumped up them as soon as she saw them and both the man and the boy were delighted. There was no doubt they would have her and the deal was done. We even threw in her feeding bowl and favourite toy. I felt it wiser not to have those memories there when she was gone. She climbed into the car with them, with not even a look back, and they drove away, and Josie whispered "Goodbye Scotty" and cried and cried and cried and I hugged her and wept also.

Life without Scotty was certainly quieter, and much easier for Josie. She had her regular checkup with her, now our, doctor and all was well on course for 10th March. As well as her craving for the fruit I could bring her from work, and that was only available when the canning line was canning fruit, she had a craving for oranges and I would often bring her home five or six and she would nearly devour them all in one night. She didn't go far now and I was reluctant to take her on the scooter, remembering our spill of last winter, so it was up to others to visit her. Her mum did often, and Christine once or twice, and other friends she had made at the factory but mostly she spent the day alone with just the geese for company.

Weekends, we caught the bus to North Walsham to do our weekly shop. Whilst there I borrowed a book from the library on the raring of poultry, particularly geese. I knew from it that this was the time that mating would take place and to look out for signs of nesting. The weather still seemed incompatible to such activity for there were still patches of snow amongst the grass tussocks in their pen and not knowing what to expect I anticipated nest making amongst the grass, though common sense told me it was still too cold for such things. Josie never went in the pen. It was left to me and although I now knew how to handle them by distracting them with one hand and grasping the neck with the other it doesn't work with three at once and their beaks are pretty vicious. Usually I'd choose to go in when they were on the other side of the pen. It was on one of these forays that I came across an egg lying on the ground. It didn't look like an egg should look and when I picked it up it was soft. It had no shell at all. I was disappointed because I thought all our hopes were going to come to naught. I mentioned this to Tosh who was of course the poultry expert and he said it was due to lack of lime in the soil and I should throw all my egg shells in with them plus some grit if I could get some. So this we did and hoped this would solve the problem. I kept a closer eye on them from now on but no resemblance of a nest appeared anywhere and no more soft eggs, and then one day I noticed one of the geese apparently pulling grass over what appeared to be a dip in the ground. Then she left and wandered off. I decided to investigate and going to the place where I'd seen her I moved the grass away which was still covered in frost and there to my amazement were six eggs all with hard shells. So this was what they called a nest, just a dip in the frozen soil. I quickly covered them up again and got out of there as the parents returned. I broke the news to Josie who was as excited as I was. So now we were on course for our first goslings. But were the eggs fertile? was the next question. According to the book there was a test you could carry out. You put them into a bucket of warm water and if they sank they weren't and if they floated they were. So I decided to try it. I did it outside the pen two eggs at a time and found that only three passed the test for fertility. I put them all back but kept one of the infertile ones and hoped the geese wouldn't notice, for at this stage I didn't know if the two geese were sharing a nest or if there was another stash hidden somewhere. The reason for keeping one was to eat it. I'd heard that geese eggs are nutritious and if we weren't going to get an offspring from it we might as well eat it. In keeping with being a 'son of the soil' in this case 'boil', 8 minutes approximately, I faced my first boiled goose egg. It was too big for an eggcup so I used a cup and proceeded to try and open it. This was difficult because the shells are very hard but I eventually managed it and found it was just about right. The yolk was more orange than yellow but there was nothing wrong with the taste and I had a very good breakfast from it. I couldn't persuade Josie to try it though. I'm not sure she approved, eating potential offspring, and anyway she still had difficult mornings with eating.

We didn't know how long the eggs had been there but one of the geese was incubating them. Everyday she turned them over, apparently so the chick wouldn't stick to the shell and then she sat there for the necessary period. Armed with my instruction manual I watched for signs of birth. The book said that sometimes a chick needs help out of the shell because it is so hard and I was ready to be midwife if needed. I checked whenever the mother left and eventually I saw signs of a hole appearing in one of the eggs. Carefully I removed little bits of shell around the hole till I could see movement then I left it to finish the job. The mother returned and renewed her vigil. Opinions are varied on whether to remove babies from their mothers or not. Some say that due to the clumsy gait of the birds they can easily tread on their young and kill them. Also there are so many predators, i.e. rats and sparrowhawks that their chances of survival are minimal anyway, so for protection they should be removed and cared for. Others go with the theory that the species has survived well enough without us all these years so they're quite capable of continuing to do so. I went with the modernist theory and when the next day the chick was finally free and the mother had left it for a brief while I gathered it up and took it indoors. It was still in the early stages with wet feathers and a rather drowned look and I put it in a box with a blanket near the fire and hung an infrared lamp above it to keep it warm. We watched it closely for movement and sure enough after a while it began to fluff up and move around. We provided water, which it immediately spilt, and food of some kind. I can't remember what now, probably bread crumbs or crushed cereals or something similar. In a day it had doubled in size because of its fluffed up plumage and it began to wander. Josie had to be very careful because it adopted her as its mother and followed her everywhere. At night we put it safely into it's box under the warm lamp.

Two days later we woke to find it had died in the night. Once again Josie was faced with loss and I did my best to comfort her. We had no idea why it had died and when I felt the bed under the lamp it was nice and warm so it wasn't the cold. We never knew if we had done anything wrong or not, and to add to our frustration none of the other eggs hatched out either. Our hopes of a goose flock had quickly faded.

Chapter 25

It must have been about this time that the first feelings of dissatisfaction crept in and I was forced to think of our future. The present was great. I loved my wife, my home, and my job but soon I would be a family man and doubts began to creep in about whether or not I was doing the best for them. Where would I be in 5 years time? 10 years time? There was Tosh's job of course when he decided to retire but there was nowhere else to go in the company. I suspected that all of the management were probably graduates and what I had learnt about the job was Westwick taught. Plus I didn't think that Tosh got the credit for what he did for the company. Would I fare any better. Even if I thought about doing the same job somewhere else their methods would probably be totally different to ours. And there was the element of secrecy in the frozen food industry which I've already mentioned. Too many suspicions between company and company existed that such a transfer was unlikely.

All these thoughts I kept to myself, for Josie was near her time for delivery and all our thoughts needed to be centred on that momentous and exciting event. The severe weather was over but March is still a cold month and we needed to make sure that all the warm clothing for a baby was ready. Josie had knitted a few warm cardigans that would come in handy and it gave her something to do during the winter but we needn't have worried about clothes for they were the main gift that was given for a birth. I was fortunate enough to come across someone who made things out of wicker. She was displaying her craft and amongst the many things she had made was a really beautiful woven crib. The inside was lined with a white material and there was a mattress to match. I was won over as soon as I saw it and bought it immediately for £4. I took it home proudly to show Josie who was equally delighted with it.

The tenth of March came and went, and the next day and nothing happened. Josie's case was packed and ready, for the doctor had told her that if the baby hadn't arrived a week after it was due she was to take herself to North Walsham Cottage Hospital, where Melanie's baby Cindy was born. I felt helpless because I was at work and couldn't be of much use, but fortunately Fiona was always on hand, even though she was restricted by looking after Cindy. She had found someone she could rely on to look after her occasionally but she was of course wary of leaving her after the last time.

A week later Josie caught the bus to North Walsham and presented herself at the hospital. I knew she was going in and that evening I rode over to see her. There was only one other woman in her ward and the staff was hardly visible so I stayed with her for a while. She was in good spirits but couldn't wait for it to be over.

"The doctor says he is going to start me off tomorrow" she said.

"Well that's good anyway" I said, as eager as her to see things through. Finally the sister in charge dismissed me and I told Josie I would ring her the next morning from work to see what was happening. We kissed. I told her I loved her, and the baby, and left for home.

That night I had a very restful sleep. Each night leading up to this one I had been aware that Josie could go into labour at anytime and this meant that neither of us slept well. Now that Josie was in good hands and knowing that nothing would be done till the morning I was able to sleep undisturbed. Next morning I went to work as usual and everyone was anxious for news. I used the lab phone to ring the hospital and ask how things were. The reply came as a total shock.

"Mr Clark your wife gave birth to a son this morning at 5a.m. 6lb 12 ounces. Both mother and baby are fine."

I nearly dropped the phone. Tosh and Steve were there waiting for news with the two women. "What is it?" Tosh asked.

"She's had it already!" I said stunned. "I've got a son!"

They were all as excited as I was. "Off you go then" prompted Tosh "she'll be waiting for you. Congratulations. And give Josie our best wishes" and Meg Phyllis and Steve added their best wishes too. I hurriedly changed from my coat, hat and wellys, put on my road gear and went for my bike. Before I could ride away however Tosh appeared with a bunch of daffodils he'd picked from the office garden. "Here, give her these from all of us" I grinned and thanked him, put them in my cycle pannier and road off.

    I was a mixture of excitement and guilt, 'a son' it was unbelievable. "*We had a son!*" But I felt guilty knowing that whilst Josie was going through the business of having him I was sleeping soundly, blissfully unaware of what was going on. I managed to arrive without an accident, which was surprising considering my thoughts were anywhere but on the road and I entered the hospital with my bunch of daffodils. Josie was alone in the ward, alone that is but for the cot, which now contained our son. She was sitting up waiting and we embraced and kissed and, then I looked at our child. What could I say? He was bonny and beautiful and I thanked Josie and praised her for all she'd been through. Had it been difficult? I asked. She said "Not too bad" but for much of the night she had been alone in the ward as the labour progressed and she had sung to herself "Fools rush in where angels fear to tread." This made me feel even more guilt for not being there for her and I told her so.

    "But it's all over now, and it was worth it wasn't it?"

    "Oh yes" I replied "it was certainly worth it."

    I didn't need to inform her parents because they had also rung the hospital and heard the good news. Steve had informed Melanie at work so now the whole family knew, and everyone at work would by bush telegraph. I held my son and felt very insecure at the responsibility of such a tiny life, which was now ours to take care of. Later in the morning her parents arrived and I stepped back to let them enthuse over their second grandchild. I had yet to inform my parents so eventually I left them saying I would call in again in the evening.

Chapter 26

Who would have imagined how much could happen to one person in two years. I came alone, and now we were three. Steve's joke at our wedding 'Two warm fronts converging followed by a little son' had been a prophecy. Well here he was and we called him James, Peter Clark. J.P.Clark, well maybe he would be a J.P. one day, someone important anyway, we were sure of it. We called him James because we liked the name, and he must never be Jimmy or Jim, and Peter after his grandfather. My parents were delighted and would come and see him as soon as they could. I called to see Josie every evening and like Melanie before her, she got thoroughly bored waiting to come home. She handled James extremely well, or so it seemed to me, whilst I was put off by his vulnerability and total dependence on us. Later she admitted to me that in truth she was scared out of her mind at the thought of sole responsibility when she came home and I was at work. The day they came home we hired a taxi, door to door service, no waiting for buses on such an important day.

I had done my best to keep the house tidy during her absence and had built the wood stock up from our free source. I had used the minimum of heat for myself, choosing rather to go to bed early after my hospital visits than light a fire for such a short time. I knew that heating would be essential when they came home. Fortunately that day was a Saturday and I was there for them. The house was clean and warm and I'd done the shopping. This was a learning weekend for both of us. James seemed permanently hungry and had no idea of bedtime as we knew it. Josie breast fed him at first but his demand was so great that home brew had to give way to 'Cow and Gate'. This required an assistant, me, which gave a new meaning to 'nightcap'. But we got through, as parents do and were pleased when visitors called, especially those who had served an apprenticeship in child care. How we managed without a telephone though I'll never know, but we did. It required planning and foresight every time we went out. Last minute calls just didn't exist. Fortunately the Co-op at North Walsham delivered groceries and you could give them a list of your next week's requirements when they came.

Like James, Josie regained her appetite and with it her strength, for nine months of sickness had been a drain on her. When she could she'd take James out in the March/April sunshine in his pram, but sadly the walk to her parents' house was too far. On the odd occasion she would walk to Worstead by way of the Arch and turn right, and meet her mum there with Cindy and they would spend a little time together before each going their separate ways home. Of course she also visited the factory to show off our offspring, making it near lunchtime when people were free to ogle and compliment. This way too she could have a drink in the canteen and renew acquaintances.

Big changes were taking place in the factory. Whether it was down to Karl's work or just normal progress, the method of freezing peas was going to be changed. The term 'freeze dried' applied to a belt along which peas were virtually bounced along in sub zero blasts to emerge two minutes later frozen solid and ready to be packed. The same method could also be used for sprouts and broad beans, anything that didn't fall apart in the process, which obviously ruled out soft fruit. The engineers were busy getting it all ready in time for the Pea season. Changes of this nature were inevitable in a fast developing industry.

Similarly, change had dominated my thoughts for the last few weeks and I thought it only fair to involve Josie in my concerns for the future. She had no strong views on the matter for or against but asked me what else I could do if not my present job, and reminded me that a change of job would mean a change of home for this was a tied house. I had realised that and promised that I wouldn't do anything silly but would she mind if I looked into the possibility of training for a profession.

It would of course have to be one which provided a grant, for I couldn't do it otherwise. She said there was no harm in looking and we left it at that.

Lack of sleep is the price one pays for bringing children into the world and James was no exception in inflicting this on us. We suffered it in the same way as parents always have, but add to that the greeting of the dawn by three honking geese everyday and tempers were bound to fray. Nobody had warned us of this and often, just as we three had fallen asleep after a difficult night, we were awakened by these sentinels of the sunlight. It also worried us that this dawn chorus may also be irritating our neighbours. We hadn't had much luck with our domestic animals and to be honest the geese had made little difference to our piece of scrubland. It was already showing signs of being just as prolific as before. We decided that our future wasn't in geese and that they too had to go.

My parents hadn't been over yet to see James, so one Saturday we took him to see them. Josie enjoyed showing him off and they loved him too. Whilst there I took the opportunity to visit Norwich Reference Library. I wanted to see what opportunities were open for such as me to get a training grant in a profession. After an hour, the only ones I could find were for Teaching or as an Assistant Preventative Officer in the Customs Service. I jotted down the relevant information and left.

Back home later that day I informed Josie of what I had discovered.

"I have enough qualifications for both and both give a grant for training. The problem with the customs is, the main jobs are at ports and airports, whereas for teaching there is a college at Keswick near Norwich, which trains teachers. What do you think?"

"John" she said "It's your decision. James and I will go with you whatever you decide but it would be better not to go too far. But you have to be absolutely sure this is what you want to do. It's a big decision."

Of course I wasn't sure. How can one be? My motives were right. I was sure of that, but was this the way to go?

"Why don't you find out about it?" she said "It can't do any harm, just asking."

We got rid of the geese, back to the person who sold them to us. We made a loss but we weren't bothered. He was sorry they hadn't quite worked out and putting them back in his car boot drove away. I was now busy planting early potatoes, cabbages and cauliflowers. This year I would win the prize at the show. James was putting on weight and the weather still had that Spring chill. I had received information about teaching and had followed it up by applying for an interview. Now it was up to them. Josie had said nothing to her parents about our possible move. After all, nothing had yet been decided. She didn't know how they'd react if we did move.

The first weeks of motherhood were not without tears. Josie had days of depression when she felt she couldn't cope but my coming home usually managed to reassure her as I assumed responsibility for James in the evenings and together we would sit in the warmth of our upstairs lounge after dinner, reading or watching television, and life felt pretty good. But the thought of the long hours and shift work that would be on us in two months time which would deprive us of this pleasure gave impetus to my search for an alternative. The other motivating factor being that no holidays could be taken in the summer, thus forever denying us any hope of family holidays in the best weather. The good news was that Steve and Melanie were talking about getting married which certainly met with Fiona's approval. Melanie was now 18 and Steve 26. They broke the news to us first on one of their visits. They frequently called in, preferring our company to the girls' parents, we being of similar age and having more in common.

I was called for an interview to Keswick Hall College of Education, just south of Norwich, at the beginning of May. I took a day off for personal reasons and attended. The College was set in beautiful grounds and I thought how conducive to study it was. The interview went well in front of three of the college staff and I was told that I'd hear from them shortly, after they'd decided.

It was about this time that we heard of the sad news of the death of Scotty. Apparently she had hurt her back very badly when trying to jump a ditch and had had to be put to sleep. This upset us both as it did their present owners who like us had become very fond of her. It was a very sad end for such a lively dog.

We made the most of May. The lawn in front of the house had grown well and Josie enjoyed somewhere nice to sit where she could get out of doors in the sun. The small windows in the house made it a dark place to be. She would lay James on a blanket on the grass with her when it was warm whilst I would potter about in the garden, then we'd change roles and I'd spend time with him or we'd both just share the pleasure of being with each other.

The factory was gearing up for the busy season though already much was going on. As in previous years early crops were being processed and the number of workers were beginning to increase. Broad beans were the crop in at the present and it gave opportunity to try out the new freezing method in anticipation of the pea harvest. I had a good crop of broad beans in my own garden from an autumn sowing and decided to use the skills I'd learnt by preserving them in kilner jars. The procedure was the same. You put them in jars, added a hot brine solution, screwed on the lids and cooked them in the oven. By this method I was able to store surplus beans for the future and hoped to do the same with other produce. From the fields around us we could tell that the peas were nearly ready for harvest and knew our time together would soon be curtailed as the viners would begin their rampage. But before then I heard from the College. I had been accepted to start training at the end of September. Josie was prepared for it and accepted it as the best we could do, but was naturally worried about where we would live. I told her not to worry, we would find something, but at this stage I didn't know where. We both agreed not to tell anyone just yet about our news.

    The same arrangement as last year was employed by Steve and myself. I took the early shift, he the night shift. Thus I had almost all day to explore the housing problem. My sister Karen had agreed to spend a week of her annual holiday with us to help Josie and keep her company in the evenings. During that time she made it clear that her interest in Steve had not diminished since the day of our wedding when he had made such a fuss over both bridesmaids and said she would like to see him again. When we pointed out that he and Melanie were practically engaged she just smiled and said "But they're not yet are they?" I knew this spelled trouble and warned her not to cause any. Steve and Melanie were our contact with Fiona and Peter. One afternoon he called round with some clothes for James that Fiona had sent. Of course Karen was delighted to see him and used all her female charm to make him notice her. She was an attractive girl anyway and she knew it. When Steve announced he was on his way to North Walsham on an errand she immediately asked if she could come with him as she'd never been there and would love to see it. Josie stepped in to say that she shouldn't bother him but he said it was no bother and he'd be delighted to show her around. And so they set off. Two hours later they returned and Karen said she'd had a lovely time and even gave him a little kiss before he drove off to pick up Melanie from work. At the end of the week Karen returned to Norwich and we heaved a sigh of relief that a potential problem had been averted.

    About a week later I was about the factory on business when a very worried and angry Melanie confronted me. "What's up Melanie?" I asked, "You look troubled"

"I am John" she said. "And I don't know what I should do."

"Well tell me about it, if you think it will help."

"I found a letter in Steve's car. It was from your sister Karen to Steve." I immediately felt trouble brewing. She went on. "John ....it was a love letter. She sounded totally infatuated with him. Is there something I should know John?

What's going on?" She was near to tears and I tried my best to tell her it was all in Karen's mind that she had nothing to fear from my sister and that Steve loved her, Melanie, very much.

"But have they been seeing each other or what?" This was when I made my big mistake by saying that as far as I knew the only time he'd seen her since the wedding was when she stayed at ours for a week and he gave her a lift to North Walsham. Me and my big mouth.

"I didn't know about that!" she retorted loudly.

"*Oh dear*" I thought, "*We've been here before*"

"He never mentioned it."

"Because there was nothing to mention, obviously."

"Apparently Karen thinks otherwise."

"Look" I said, "Have you mentioned any of this to Steve?"

"No! Of course not. I thought I'd speak to you first."

"Right. When did you see the letter?"

"Yesterday."

"And where is it now?"

"Where I found It."

"Well I suggest you give Steve a chance to explain. I'm sure it means nothing to him, and I know he loves you." With some reservations she decided to follow my advice and I left her to carry on with her work. When Steve came on shift at eleven I hesitated about talking to him about it. After all it was between Melanie and him but then the problem was solved because he said "John, I've had this letter from your sister Karen and it's, well.., it's rather difficult to say, but to put it frankly, she seems to have a bit of a crush on me."

"Oh really?" I said innocently. "and how do you feel about her?"

"I don't feel anything about her, well not in that way. She's a nice girl and all that but that's where it ends." I was so pleased with what he said that I could have kissed him myself but that would have been misinterpreted too. "I didn't want Melanie to find out. What do you think I should do?"

"Leave it to me Steve" I told him. "Give the letter to me and I'll have a word. Hopefully you won't have anymore trouble.

What it is to be irresistible." We both laughed and he gave me the letter and set off on his rounds of the factory.

The next day I told Melanie that Steve had volunteered the information and I was going to deal with it and she had nothing to fear and to treat it as if it never happened. She was so relieved and thanked me though I insisted I'd done nothing, just listened. She looked much happier when I left her.

Chapter 27

Enquiries on the home front gave little hope of being able to rent anything easily. One had to be on the spot, at the time, in order to procure the few properties that became available. The best bet was to buy. The cheapest property was around the £1600 mark and a 10% deposit was usually needed. This was impossible in our circumstances. We had told my parents what we planned to do for they were on the spot and could possibly help us find somewhere.

On one of my visits home I had confronted Karen and put her in the picture concerning Steve. She refused to believe that he didn't care for her unless she heard from him herself but when I gave her back her letter and said "Why would he give me this if he cherished thoughts of you in that way?" She had to believe what I had told her. Like Melanie before her I found myself telling her that she'd find someone someday and she'd soon forget about Steve.

Once again a sea of fresh, Irish faces were arriving to earn their tuition fees and were set to work on the various tasks about the factory. Some of them looked so young and had never worked as hard as they did here. Some of them got very homesick after a couple of weeks and I put it to Josie that it would be nice to have a few over for tea one day just to get them away from the Spartan conditions of their lives in a Nissan hut where all they had was a bed and no home comforts. She was willing to give it a try, perhaps on a Sunday afternoon but only when I was on nights so I could spend the evening with them. So we postponed the idea till July.

Meanwhile a message got through to me via my parents that an aunt of mine was willing to lend us the deposit on a house. She had been at our wedding and admired what I was trying to do. This was great news and I broke it to Josie. "Now we can look anywhere for a house" I told her "though it won't be a palace, but at least it will be ours" This news cheered Josie who could now see our move being a reality. Before, there was every chance that it might fall through. I thanked my aunt most sincerely and said I would only accept her kind offer if she let me pay it back with the current rate of interest. She agreed but put no time limit on repayment. So began requests to Estate Agents to send us details of properties in our price range.

The peas now flowed through the tunnel at a phenomenal rate, straight into catering size polythene bags, then into boxes and into freezer storage. Because few people had domestic freezers we didn't pack in small bags as one sees in the supermarkets today but mainly for caterers. That would come later when freezers were as common as ovens in the kitchen.

I felt guilty about not telling Tosh I was leaving, but I had no way of knowing how the management would take it and if they would ask me to leave earlier if they found out. Not that I thought they would for they wouldn't be able to train anyone else in the time and they needed me through the summer season. For the same reason I hesitated to tell Fiona and Peter for Melanie might let it slip. But they were Josie's parents after all so we agreed we had to tell them. When?, was the next problem for I didn't want to leave Josie to do it on her own. There was no public transport to get us there and with the baby the scooter was no use, and what was true for us was equally true for Fiona who cared for Cindy all day. It was a problem which we found difficult to resolve. In the end it resolved itself. Being a farm worker, Peter often had use of a farm vehicle and one Saturday morning he was taking Fiona and Cindy to North Walsham to do some shopping. They passed by our house, so naturally called in. This was the ideal time to tell them, so we did. They were both quiet for a while when we had finished, then Fiona spoke.

"A teacher eh? Well that's a good job anyway. We've never had a teacher in the family."

"And we'll only be living in Norwich" I said "That's not far, and who knows after training I might even be able to get a job around here."

"Well you've got to do what you think is best" added Peter.

"And you can visit whenever you like" prompted Josie "and we'll visit you."

The niceties over, they then pushed us on hard facts, like money and housing etc. and we did our best to allay their fears. We told them about my aunt's offer and showed them the details of houses we were interested in from the estate agents. When they were sure that at least we'd thought it all out they felt better than they had initially and though it felt as if I was taking their daughter and grandchild from them, albeit only about 12 miles, they appreciated that it was probably an upward move. Peter even agreed to bring Fiona over one day next week so she could baby-sit the two babies and we could look at some houses. We were grateful for that and accepted their kind offer.

Steve and Melanie announced their engagement that weekend and no one was happier than Josie and me. He bought her a diamond ring and, as they had done with us, the family had a special tea to celebrate. They too were anxious to marry as soon as they could find somewhere to live. It had not escaped our notice that soon there would be a house to rent not far away but as yet Steve knew nothing about our future plans.

True to their word Peter brought Fiona with Cindy to look after James and we made an early start to Norwich. We had three houses to look at, each was a terraced house with a small back garden and even smaller front garden. There wasn't much to choose between them, they were in long terraces of many years standing and after all the space we had been used to they felt cramped. It was all a matter of which was in the best structural and decorative state, and which was the most convenient for me to get to work. All were on good bus routes and had easy access to the city centre. In the end we opted for one and returned to the estate agent to talk business. We made an offer for it and the agent said he would have to contact us about the result. So we returned to Westwick. I was aware of what we were giving up for such a confined space and how difficult it was for a country girl like Josie to adapt but I reasoned that this was only a temporary move till I was qualified, then we would move to something bigger and better. Josie on the other hand surprised me by saying there were more buses, more parks, more places to visit and definitely more shops. For a country girl this was all a new experience and would not be the trauma I had expected.

I phoned the next day and heard that our offer had been accepted and we commenced the procedure of purchasing. Several other phone calls got the ball rolling and later I remember walking around our garden, noticing the rockeries we had built with discarded stone now covered in blue forget-me-nots, vegetables growing lush and green in the reclaimed ground, the apple trees once again full of fruit, that area of uncultivated land that I had hopes and plans for but which would now have to be left to someone else, and yes, I did have doubts, lots of them.

Chapter 28

With the coming of mid July I was once again on nights and we shared the late afternoons and evenings together. I brought up the subject of inviting a few of the students home for afternoon tea and Josie agreed. It would have to be on a Sunday. Somehow it seemed the right day to do it even though every day was virtually alike. Many of the students were Catholics and went to mass anyway so it was special for them already. I had got to know several of them through work connected with the lab and I invited them round if they weren't working at the time. They were pleased with the invitation and I told them where we lived and I would expect them anytime after 3p.m. This meant that I would need to be up in good time to welcome them and Josie said she would see that I was.

On the day, four of them turned up: Patrick, Sean, Brendan and Daniel. All had made an attempt to dress up and they presented Josie with a small gift of a cloth made of Irish linen. Where they got it from I don't know but it was much appreciated. We sat in the small lounge, bringing chairs from the kitchen to fit the number and we chatted about work and their homes and families and even touched on religion and the troubles back home. They were themselves a mixture of Catholics, Baptists and Presbyterians and had no animosity between themselves and I thought how promising that was for the province of Northern Ireland for these were the men of the future who hopefully could influence the thinking of the province and bring a peaceful end to the conflict. They were themselves training as engineers, physicists, architects and geologists and they explained how a pound earned here could be worth twice as much back home. They made a fuss of James and even watched a bit of television for they hadn't seen one for weeks. Josie had prepared a simple tea of sandwiches and cake with lots of tea to drink and we continued chatting till the early evening when they said their good byes. Two were ready for sleep having worked already, and two were due to start that evening. They expressed their gratitude and said it reminded them of home and went on their way. I hoped that wouldn't mean they would be more homesick than they were, rather that it would give them a boast to finish their season with us.

August came and I finally had to tell Tosh that I was leaving. It was the hardest thing to do, for I felt I was letting him down personally. The factory could get someone else, that was life, but Tosh had been good to me, had personally enabled us to get married, had found us a house, had taken delight in our child, and shown concern in our novice beginnings in house management. I broke the news to him one morning when he came on shift just before I went home. He was surprised, naturally enough, and I felt, a little disappointed, then he told me that his father had been a teacher so he had some respect for what I had chosen to do. I told him I would be there for the season, not expecting to leave till the end of September. I felt that was some compensation for him, some gratitude for what he had done for me. This way I thought we would be able to leave amicably. There was no animosity on his part which made it even harder to have broken this news to him. But the deed was done and it was left to me to serve out my notice. I returned home and told Josie the outcome. She knew I wasn't happy about it but it had been inevitable. Tomorrow, I expected, everybody would know.

The purchase of the house was going well. Because we were first time buyers we brought no chain with us so that made it easier. We planned to move late September, a week before I started College giving us time to settle in and do any jobs that needed doing to the house, like decorating. I knew living on a grant wouldn't be easy, especially after the low rent we were paying here, but I had anticipated, that during the long holidays from College, I would be able to work to supplement our income.

I was glad, after all, that I hadn't told Steve about our plans because the first thing Tosh said when he arrived at work was

"John tells me he's leaving. Did you know?" And in all honesty he answered "No. I didn't know. Where's he going?" So Tosh told him what I had said. It was left to me later that night to explain that the reason we hadn't told him was to avoid putting him in the position where he would have had to keep a secret from Tosh and we didn't think that was fair. I then suggested that when we left, our house would be available, and as he was really senior to me, at least in years of service, he had an even better chance of obtaining it than I had had. He certainly saw the sense in that and he said he would discuss it with Melanie next day.

Melanie was none too pleased that no one had told her we were moving, as a sister she thought she had a right to know, but we finally managed to convince her that it had always been possible that our plans might not have come to fruition and then the fewer people who knew the better. And then the thought that our leaving might be the means of her finding somewhere to live, calmed her down somewhat.

Plans moved on swiftly now. My leaving was soon general knowledge. Many expressed sadness that I was going, especially May and Phyllis who were going to miss me. They didn't like change and took pride in looking after the men in the lab. But in the same way that I had been accepted when I first arrived, nobody criticised my decision. Tosh had informed Rupert Beard but he never spoke to me. There was nothing new in that. Christine said she was sorry we were going. She would miss Josie and James, for she had kept in touch. A couple of weeks later we heard that she too was pregnant and her longed for wish was granted. Tosh made enquiries of the Chairman about the house on Steve's behalf and his reply was "It's all one and the same to me" so Melanie and Steve were as happy about it as we had been before them, and it meant that we wouldn't have to say goodbye completely. They made plans for their wedding sometime in Autumn.

I finished my night shift in September and had two weeks on days before leaving, enabling me to say my goodbyes proper to those at work. Josie brought James to the factory for the last time so she could say goodbye properly. The final day eventually arrived. There was no great ceremony. I was glad about that, just a cordial farewell to everybody in the lab, mutual thanks for friendship, and best wishes for the future, then I surrendered my green hat and white coat and bade the factory goodbye.

The day of our moving arrived. We had a small van. Our few belongings wouldn't fill a big one. Some things were left for Steve and Melanie including the curtains for after all those were the windows they fitted. It didn't take long to pack, then we locked the door and left the key in a prearranged place. The van drove off to be met by members of my family who would oversee the unpacking. We had to catch a bus. We stood and surveyed the scene, Josie holding James and I remembered her saying to me when we first stood here "We will be happy here won't we John?" and I had said "We'll have a damn good try" Well we had been happy. We'd tried many things, some successful, some not, but yes we had been happy. It was a sad day for us both. This had been our first home. It had nurtured us through our first sixteen months. We had learnt to live together. We had had our first child here and sadly he would only know about it through us or on future visits. That last thought comforted us as the bus arrived and we climbed aboard and left. We watched the house disappear from view as the bus carried us to our future life.

Looking back on all that had happened to me those three years I can honestly say that they were three of the happiest years of my life and for me those memories will always be 'Frozen in Time'.

The End

Notes on the story

The cherry orchards are no longer there. Neither is the Arch. It was demolished in 1981. A sign now stands in its place to commemorate it. On it is also a sheep to remind us of the nearness of Worstead and its importance to the woollen industry, and cherries as a reminder of the cherry orchards. The factory still stands but is now owned by Heinz. Mr. Alexander was subsequently knighted. There are no shops at Westwick or Worstead now and the old village hall has been demolished and a new one built behind the New Inn public house. The house at Old Hall Farm still stands but is now in private hands and is currently being restored as one property. The apple trees are gone and the front is now all down to lawn. Much of the cowshed has been demolished. The church of St. Mary still dominates the area as it has done for 8 centuries.

Since 1965 there has been a festival held in Worstead every year taking place in the last weekend of July. The Worstead Festival is the largest village festival in Norfolk attracting around 25,000 visitors.

Printed in the United Kingdom
by Lightning Source UK Ltd.
103606UKS00001B/34-45